Robin Hood
The Wrath of God

DAVID PILLING

"These Bishoppes and Archebyshoppes, them ye shall beat and bind…" – the Lytell Geste of Robyn Hode, c.1470.

CONTENTS

1.

Sherwood Forest, Nottinghamshire,

The Great North Road that cut through the forest was wide enough for sixteen men to ride abreast. Today, on the stretch between Newark-on-Trent and Retford, it was required to bear merely one.

This man, a Cistercian monk, kept his dappled grey pony at a rather swifter pace than the dignity of his order allowed. One reason for his haste was fear of the outlaws that lurked in the depths of Sherwood. Another was the content of the letter he carried in his saddle-bag, written and sealed by the hand of the High Sheriff of Nottinghamshire.

The Sheriff, practical man that he was, had refused the monk's request for an armed escort. "That will alert every brigand in the forest," he said. "Some of them are bold rogues, and will not hesitate to try their luck against soldiers. I would have to despatch at least twenty riders to see you safe, and cannot spare the men. Your best chance is to slip through the forest alone. One poor priest isn't much of a temptation."

These words were little comfort to the monk, a naturally timid man who had chosen the cloister as the surest way of ensuring a peaceful life. He paid the requisite lip-service to God, and muttered the Latin forms as well as any of his brethren, but possessed little in the way of actual piety.

Fear lent conviction to his faith, such as it was. He babbled prayers and clutched the little crucifix around his neck, his eyes flickering from side to side, watching anxiously for any sign of life among the trees that clustered thick beyond the roadside.

His pale, freckled hands shook on the bridle as something rustled in the woods to his left. He cruelly raked his pony's flanks with his spurs, urging the beast from a fast canter to a gallop.

"Faster, damn you," he rasped, crouching low over her neck.

The pony whickered at such brutal treatment. She was in danger of turning a hoof, for the roads were in a poor state, but the monk cared little. He was blind to anything except the need to get out of this valley of death, and unconvinced that the Lord walked by his side.

A green-fletched arrow flitted out of the woods and slapped into his pony's neck. She screamed and skidded to a halt, throwing up a spray of loose earth and stones.

The monk was no great horseman, and not able to regain control of his mount. Desperate to stay in the saddle, he flung his arms around her neck, but she reared back on her haunches and shook him loose. He was thrown into the air and landed on his side with rib-cracking impact.

Stunned, he lay prone for a few seconds, groaning feebly. It was agony to move. Pains like red-hot needles stabbed through his left side.

"My ribs," he whined, "Christ save me, my ribs are broken."

He heard male voices, low and soothing as they tried to calm his pony.

"I am sorry I had to shoot her," said one, "she was going at a fair clip, and you didn't want the monk hurt."

That was encouraging. Stifling his moans of pain, the monk dared to open his eyes a fraction.

A trio of tall, sunburned men were trying to catch his pony, and being led a merry dance as she careered and bucked wildly about the road. They looked like foresters, garbed all in faded greens and browns, but their coarse, battered faces hinted at something darker.

Another man stood nearby, watching the performance with his hands tucked into his heavy sleeves. The monk's heart leaped at the sight of him. He wore the brown habit of a monk: soiled and patched, true, and his tonsure was shamefully overgrown, but still he appeared to be a fellow man of God.

"Brother," the monk gasped, lifting his right hand to get the other's attention. "Help me to my feet, in Christ's name. I am hurt."

The hedge-priest glanced down at him. "You look whole enough to me," he said disdainfully. "Get up, man. Don't grovel in the dust. You will soil those fine robes."

Feeling a little less relieved – there was something about the priest's tone and narrow, bony features he didn't trust – the monk struggled to rise, wincing at every fresh burst of pain in his ribs.

The foresters had his pony under control now, more or less, and one of them was trying to work the arrow out of her neck. The air turned black with their curses as she struggled to break free.

"You must protect me, brother," said the monk, almost bent double with pain, his eyes misted with tears, "protect me from these thieves."

"My friends can be a little rough," replied the other, "but they respect men of the cloth. Blame yourself for your hurts. If you had not been riding at such a foolish pace, we would have called on you to halt."

"Yours is a wealthy order," he added, stepping closer and holding out his hand, "and I'm afraid we must relieve you of your purse. Hand it over."

"Purse? I have none. Only a few pennies to see me safe to York."

There were deep lines scored into the corners of the priest's mouth. He looked like one who had lived a hard life, deprived of the comforts enjoyed by many churchmen, and they deepened further as he frowned. His face had a stern, ascetic quality, with something of the Old Testament prophet about it.

"You were in a hurry, then," he said, scratching his whiskery cheek, "which means you carry some message or other. What is it?"

The monk quailed before the other's grey eyes, full of steel and fire and fierce intelligence, and nerved himself to lie. "Nothing important," he said, gasping at another stab of pain, "a trifling business matter. Of no value save to the parties concerned. Certainly nothing that would interest you."

"Really? You are in error, brother. I am very much interested."

"John!" he shouted, turning to the men holding the pony, "search through the saddle-bags. There should be a letter in there somewhere. When you find it, give it to me."

The largest of the three men, a black-bearded giant with shoulders like a bull, shifted his grip on the shivering pony's neck and rifled through the leather bags hanging from her

3

saddle.

"Here," he said eventually, producing a square of parchment, folded and sealed with a red wax seal. The priest strode over to him and took the letter.

"There was nothing else?" he asked, cracking open the seal. John shook his head.

The monk watched, palpitating, as the hedge-priest unfolded the letter and read the contents. His slender hope that the priest might be illiterate, as such men often were, died inside him.

"From his lordship the High Sheriff of Nottinghamshire, Derbyshire and the Royal Forests, no less, and written in his own hand," the priest read aloud, "he presents his compliments to his esteemed colleague, the High Sheriff of Yorkshire, and begs to inform him that…"

His voice trailed away, his lips moving soundlessly as he read on.

The priest's pale face steadily darkened. When he had finished reading, he looked up with pure rage sparkling in his eyes.

"Liar!" he cried, pointing one black-nailed finger at the monk, whose heart skipped a couple of beats. "So this letter concerned a trifling business matter, eh? Is that how you term a man's life – our master's life?"

The monk started, and tried to think of an explanation, but terror had frozen his tongue. He fell to his knees, careless of the agony in his cracked ribs, and clasped his hands in supplication.

"Please," he begged, "I am merely a messenger. I know nothing of the letter's content, or your master. The Sheriff instructed me not to read it."

"Horse shit, brother," said the priest, his voice full of icy, controlled anger, "my lord Sheriff says otherwise. He writes that you recognised our master, Robyn Hode, as he knelt at prayer in St Mary's Church. That you ran to fetch the Sheriff and his bullies, and pointed Robyn out to him."

His comrades had now lost all interest in the pony. They released her, allowing the beast to limp away, blood oozing from the wound in her neck.

"What's this?" demanded John, "Robyn has been taken?"

"Taken, and imprisoned inside Nottingham Castle," said the priest, "the Sheriff has sent this letter to Eustace of Lowdham, offering to try the prisoner, or send him under guard to York."

"Robyn should never have gone to Nottingham," said another of the robbers, a thin-faced man with hair the colour of scraped carrot, "but he might still be at liberty, if not for this quaking little turd."

He scowled at the monk, who was having trouble retaining control of his bladder. All four men looked hard at him. They were killers, he had no doubt of that, and would snuff out his life without a qualm.

The priest scrunched the letter into a ball. "God has thrown this man into our path," he said thoughtfully, "else we would still be ignorant of Robyn's capture. Therefore God means us to forget recent quarrels and aid our master."

Littiljohn coloured. "Maybe so," he grunted, "but what can we do? A thousand men could not storm Nottingham Castle."

"True. Something more subtle is required."

The priest carried a long knife in a sheepskin-lined sheath tucked into the rope around his waist. He slowly drew the knife and advanced on the monk.

"First," he said softly, "this one must pay for his treachery."

The monk stared in terror at the blade. He tried to form words, to beg for his life, but they stuck in his throat. His heart was skipping much too fast. Blood roared and pounded in his ears.

He groaned at a fresh explosion of pain, this time in his chest. Burning heat swarmed up his left arm. Black spots danced in front of his eyes, and he struggled for breath that suddenly would not come.

The knife had no time to touch his flesh, before the monk's heart failed and his soul was gathered unto God.

2.

York

Eustace received a letter from the King, advising him that the reinforcements he had craved for so long were finally on their way from London.

"Forty sergeants and sixty crossbowmen," he exclaimed, holding the letter up to the light, "their expenses to be defrayed and charged to the Exchequer. God's bones."

He put a hand to his temple and tried to think clearly. It was difficult, thanks to the alcohol and poppy juice sloshing through his veins. Eustace had suffered a slight arm-wound in the recent battle with the outlaws of Barnsdale. It had started to turn bad, so his doctors dosed him against the pain before cutting away the affected flesh.

Eustace was still weak from the crude operation, and obliged to walk with a stick. He was in no condition to receive unexpected missives from the king.

He turned to Alan, the captain of his garrison. The big, solid Breton was a reassuring presence, competent and efficient without resorting to excess.

"We need to make provision for a hundred men," Eustace said, "lodgings must be found for them inside the castle. Failing that, they can be billeted around the city. They will be here inside a week, so we must not tarry."

"Yes, lord," said Alan, "I can find the space. Our garrison has been depleted in recent times, so we should be able to house them all inside the castle. Why is His Majesty sending so many troops, and why now?"

Eustace looked at him warily. If Alan had a fault, it was a tendency to ask questions. "That is not your business," he said, "but since you ask, he has despatched them to aid us in the hunting of the outlaw, Robyn Hode, and his companions."

"The last we saw of Hode, he was taking shelter in Hazlewood Castle. We'll need more than a hundred men to prise him out of there."

"I know that," Eustace snapped. His head swam, and he had to reach out to steady himself against the wall.

They were talking inside a small solar chamber high in one of the towers of York keep. It was hot and stuffy in there, thanks to the fire burning merrily in the grate, and the shutters over the window. Eustace's blood had turned to ice since his operation, and he craved heat.

"He will not be able to shelter inside Hazlewood for long," he said, slowly and deliberately, "it is held by the Vavasours. Unless they eject Hode, or hand him over to me in chains, they risk incurring the displeasure of the crown."

Leaving Alan to make arrangements for the arrival of the King's men, Eustace took himself to bed. There he stayed for the next three days, visited by no-one save the occasional servant bearing meals, and his formidable wife Isabel, whom no sick-chamber or locked door could deny. She was an impatient nurse, and urged him to get back on his feet and attend to his duties without delay.

"The King has placed Fawkes de Lyon, a notable Gascon captain, in command of his men," she said – doubtless she had been rifling through her husband's correspondence again – "and you must be fit and well by the time he arrives. Think of the impression he will take back to London if he comes here expecting to meet the High Sheriff, but instead finds a pathetic, bedridden invalid."

As usual, Eustace suffered her lecture in patient silence, consoling himself with the thought that she had his best interests at heart. Just for spite, he lingered in bed longer than strictly necessary, and exaggerated his symptoms, limping around the castle and groaning loudly whenever Isabel was in earshot.

He was just starting to enjoy himself when another message arrived, this time from Nottingham. The bearer was a Cistercian monk.

In Eustace's experience the Cistercians tended to be a complacent lot, plump and wealthy and well-fed, but this one was different. Tall and spare, severe and hollow-cheeked, he had a genuinely holy look and manner about him. Eustace, who preferred his churchmen fat and genially corrupt, felt nervous in the monk's presence.

He received him in the Great Hall, and sat huddled up under several layers of blankets beside a roaring fire while the monk explained his mission. The weather was grim. Rain spat through the arrow-slit windows and ran in streams down the walls.

"My name is Brother William," said the monk, with a cursory bow, "I was despatched here by the High Sheriff of Nottingham with a letter for your lordship."

"God help us, more letters," Eustace said peevishly, "Fitz Nicholas sent you all this way without an escort?"

Ralph Fitz Nicholas was the High Sheriff of Nottinghamshire. "Yes, lord," replied Brother William with a mirthless smile, "perhaps he felt that a man travelling on his own would go unnoticed. Alas, he was mistaken. I was waylaid by outlaws in Sherwood."

He produced a folded length of parchment from his belt. "They robbed me of the few pennies I carried, and broke the seal on the letter. Happily, one of them could read a little, and saw that it was of no value. Nor was I, so they let me go on my way."

Eustace took the proffered letter and frowned suspiciously at the broken seal. "How merciful of them," he said, unfolding it, "they must have taken your horse, at least?"

"They shot the poor creature, lord. Hence," – the monk indicated the wet mud that spattered the hem of his black and white robes – "the lamentable state of my clothing. Still, the walk did me good, and reminded me of a priest's humility before God."

"Quite. You were lucky not to end up with a split throat. Perhaps they spared you out of respect for your habit."

"Perhaps, lord," Brother William said noncommittally, and stood in silence while Eustace read.

For once, it was good news. The outlaw Robert Hode had been taken at St Mary's Church and consigned to Fitz Nicholas's dungeon. Eustace had hoped the man was already dead, rotting in a ditch somewhere near Barnsdale, and was surprised to learn he had ended up in Nottingham.

Not that he cared overmuch. "So far as I'm concerned, Fitz

Nicholas may hang the man from the nearest tree, or keep him locked up in perpetuity," he said, "I wash my hands of the affair."

Brother William bowed again. "You show the wisdom of Pilate, lord," he said, with another of his odd little smiles, "I may bear your answer back to Nottingham, then?"

"Yes. Later today," replied Eustace, who wanted this unsettling man out of sight and mind as soon as possible, "I will have one of my clerks draw up the letter. In the meantime you are free to eat and drink your fill in my kitchens."

He waved the monk away, and snapped his fingers at a small page lurking in a corner of the hall. The page was the son of a local knightly family, farmed out to learn his letters and manners in a noble household. Eustace had several such wards in his care. He always struggled to remember their names.

"You," he said, beckoning the lad over, "go and fetch Master Edmund, my chief scribe. He's a white-haired old sot with a great boil on his neck."

The page scampered away to do his bidding. Eustace was left alone to enjoy a rare moment of peace and solitude. He relaxed into the padded bolster of his chair, sighing as the warmth of the fire seeped into his bones.

A thought struck him like a hammer, and he jerked upright again. "God help me," he moaned, clutching his head, "what will I say to the King's men?"

3.

Nottingham

The inn known as the Trip to Jerusalem lay at the foot of the massive outcrop that bore the weight of Nottingham Castle. A small, dingy place, always crowded to bursting in the evenings, it enjoyed some local fame for its caves, hacked out of the soft sandstone rock against which the inn was built.

Matilda disliked such drinking-holes, considering them the bane of men and the ruin of families. For her husband's sake she had agreed to enter the place in the company of Will Shakelock.

The youthful Will was thoroughly at home, and wasted no time in making the acquaintance of a group of stonemason's apprentices clustered at one end of the bar. It was barely dusk, but the boys were already half-cut, and near the end of their limited funds. Will set about buying their friendship with several rounds of ale, and winked at Matilda as he passed her a cup.

"Tuck told us to make friends, remember?" he said, "so that's what I'm doing. Keep your hood up. In this light you can pass for a man."

"Thanks for the compliment," Matilda replied sourly, taking the cup, but she knew what he meant. She kept her hair closely shorn, long hair being a nuisance in the forest, and was dressed like a man in a long tunic, hooded mantle, hose and heavy boots.

With her hood up, the mob of drunks jostling each other in the tiny taproom were unlikely to realise her sex. Not that women were barred from the inn, but any that frequented such a place were likely to be taken for whores.

The first one of these brutes to paw me, Matilda thought furiously, her hand closing about the hilt of her dagger, *will end up picking his fingers off the floor.*

She took a cautious sniff of the ale and wrinkled her nose in disgust. It was rank, stale-smelling stuff, not like the rich ale her uncle used to brew at Locksley Farm.

"This is piss," she declared. No-one heard her above the drunken babble. Will was already on his second cup, and deep in conversation with the apprentices.

They were supposed to be trying to get information, anything that might help the outlaws to rescue Robyn from the dungeons of Nottingham Castle. Littiljohn had stayed in Sherwood with the rest of the outlaws to await the return of Tuck.

Tuck had assumed control of the band after Robyn's capture. No-one elected him, but his gravitas and force of personality naturally placed him in command. It was Tuck who thought of the rescue plan. After the death of the Cistercian the outlaws had waylaid, he had taken the monk's clothes and the letter from the Sheriff of Nottingham, and declared that he would go to York, posing as the Sheriff's messenger.

"With luck, Eustace of Lowdham won't ask for Robyn to be sent to York," he had explained, "and I can return and inform the Sheriff that his prisoner can be hanged in Nottingham. I will ask to see Robyn before he dies, claiming that I wish to curse him for a priest-killer and enemy of God."

"What then?" asked Matilda, who had listened attentively. She was consumed with anxiety for her husband, if annoyed that his own folly and quick temper had placed him in danger.

"Then we kill the gaoler and get out of the castle under cover of darkness," he said with a wry smile, "simple, eh?"

He stabbed a skinny forefinger at his companions. "While I am away, I need you to find another way in and out of the castle. I can enter via the gates as an official messenger, but can hardly go out the same way with Robyn."

"When I served in the garrison, I did hear of a secret tunnel bored into the rock under the keep," said Littiljohn, "I never found anything. There is a postern gate, but it is always guarded."

Tuck looked thoughtful. "The rock is sandstone, so the tunnel may exist," he said, "a sliver of hope is better than none."

None of the outlaws could think of a better plan, so Will and Matilda had volunteered to enter Nottingham and glean whatever they could from the locals. Their mission was fraught with danger, for there was no easy way of asking casual questions about secret entrances to the castle, and they were both outlawed. Anyone could kill or capture them without risk of prosecution. Outlaws were considered vermin, with no right to life or liberty.

Matilda forced herself to drink some of the ale. It was sour and unpleasantly thick, like foul-tasting gravy, but at least provided some distraction from the sweat, stink and noise all around her.

She wiped her lips and peered around at the sea of red faces. She doubted there was a single functioning brain among them, soaked as they were in ale. Certainly no-one who might be privy to the information she needed.

Will lurched over to her. He had already indulged himself too much, and Matilda feared he might say something indiscreet.

"That man over there," he muttered thickly, swivelling his eyes to the left, "he's the cook. Talk to the cook."

"Cook?" she echoed, "what the hell are you talking about? You might have told me you can't handle your drink."

He rubbed his face and tried again. "No, no," he said, "listen. That man in the corner, he's the castle cook. Been there for years, so the lads tell me. Knows the place like the back of his hand."

Matilda had to admit that was useful. She glanced at the corner, and saw a short, grotesquely fat man seated at a round table. By the look of his enflamed features, or what could be seen of them above the mossy growth of beard, he had been wallowing in his pots for quite some time. His companion, a slightly smaller man, had given up the struggle and lay slumped with his head resting in a pool of stale beer.

"Wish me luck," she said, risking another gulp of ale to stiffen her courage, and started to push her way through the greasy pack of bodies.

She paused a moment, racking her brains for something to say. Then she leaned down close to the fat man's hairy ear.

"A word with you, master," she said in a low voice. He jumped, spilling a few drops of ale as he raised the brimming flagon to his lips, and glared up at her lividly.

"You almost made me drop my fucking beer," he snarled in

an oddly high-pitched, wheezing voice, "be thankful you didn't."

His beady little eyes narrowed as he looked Matilda up and down. "What are you, a boy-whore? I'm not interested in buggers. Piss off."

Matilda drew in a sharp breath and willed herself to be calm. "Nothing of the sort," she said, "how would you like to earn some extra money? Lots of it."

That mended the cook's manners a little. He carefully put down his flagon and regarded her with wary interest. "I'm comfortable," he said, patting his belly, "but there's always room for more. How much?"

"Two pounds," she replied, "you get a quarter of the money on agreement, and the rest when the job is done."

This was reckless. Two pounds was forty shillings, more than the average labourer could earn in two years, and almost all the money that remained to the outlaws after their flight from Barnsdale.

Matilda didn't care. Tuck had placed no limit on what she could offer, and she was desperate to get her husband back, no matter the cost.

The cook moistened his lips with his tongue. His eyes were alight with greed, but she hadn't yet landed her fish.

"That's a lot of money," he said, glancing at his dead-drunk companion, "what do I have to do for it?"

She looked around furtively, and decided to risk telling him. "I need a way in and out of the castle. A secret way."

"You're not the first to ask me that," said the cook, "but none of the others offered so much money. I suppose there's no point asking questions?"

Matilda smiled and shook her head. "None."

Nothing further was said, while the cook took a long pull from his tankard and mulled over her offer.

"Meet me here tomorrow night," he said at last, "I might be able to help you. Bring the first part of the payment."

"Tomorrow night is too soon. Make it the night after."

He looked at her sharply, his eyes narrowing as he tried to peer under her hood. "You're in a bad position to bargain. What if I went to the Sheriff right now, and told him that some green-eyed lad had tried to bribe me?"

"Not a good idea," said Matilda, holding his gaze, "I'm not alone. You would be dead before you walked five paces beyond the door."

She had started to perspire, and not just due to the heat of the packed room. It was not like her to follow up a rash offer with a foolish threat, but this man seemed her only hope of saving Robyn.

The cook smirked. "It's a while since I've been threatened. Threats don't move me very much, boy, but forty shillings is forty shillings. And I have a few debts that need paying."

Matilda almost sagged with relief. "Two nights from now, then," she said, "at Vespers."

He nodded curtly and turned away from her. Matilda took that as a signal that their conversation was over. Looking around carefully to see if anyone had been eavesdropping, she went to find Will.

4.

Nottingham Castle

The dungeon was a long, thin, rectangular hole cut into the stone under the inner ward of the castle. It was part of the subterranean warren of caves and tunnels, including storerooms and wine cellars, which formed a small, self-enclosed world in the dark beneath the world.

Robyn had been held inside the dungeon for the best part of two weeks. Rating him a dangerous prisoner, the gaoler had ordered his wrists to be fastened to the iron chains that hung from divots in the walls. The chains were heavy, and obliged him to sit on the floor with his back to the wall.

For two weeks Robyn had sat and brooded in almost total darkness. The only light came from a torch in the corridor outside, filtering through the thick bars of the gate that kept the prisoners confined. The hurts he had sustained in the sight at Saint Mary's Church were slow in healing, and left him with purple bruises on his ribs and a permanent ache in his skull.

His two fellow prisoners had languished in the dungeon for months. Their spirits and bodies were broken by the ordeal. They said little, but Robyn had gleaned enough to know how the law had abused them.

One was a petty felon, a cut-purse and house-breaker, still waiting for trial seven months after his capture. The other was a much older man, a local miller who had refused to allow a knight named Sir Peter Mauley to buy up and enclose his land. Mauley had dealt with the problem by accusing the miller of poaching, and despite a total lack of evidence succeeded in having him imprisoned. His lands, naturally, were seized by the Sheriff and bought by Mauley for less than half their annual value.

These stories made Robyn forget his own troubles and filled him with unquenchable rage. Rage sustained him, helping him to endure the dark and the cold, the dreadful stench of rotting food and unwashed bodies, urine and excrement, the giant black rats that scuttled over the filthy floor and nibbled at his flesh if he remained still for too long.

"There is no justice in England," he declared repeatedly, his chains rattling as he drew them taut, "no justice for the poor, the weak and defenceless. Our laws are sold like cows to the highest bidder."

This drew no response from his companions. They were virtually hidden in darkness, their emaciated bodies slumped, heads bowed in defeat and misery. Robyn wished he could strike a spark of defiance in them, but their fires were burned out. Only basic instincts remained, such as when the gaoler came with their dinner: a jug of mouldy water drawn from a ditch, and a pail of stale bread and mouldy cheese. Then they showed some twitches of life, and devoured the grisly repast like hungry dogs before pissing and shitting themselves where they lay.

"Filthy beasts," the gaoler would grunt, cuffing them with his ham-sized fists. He was a skinny, yellow-faced man, dressed all in soiled and shabby black, but in Robyn's mind he gradually took on the aspect of a monster. He often daydreamed of breaking free of his chains and slaughtering the gaoler like a pig, cutting his throat and leaving him to bleed to death on the floor. The futility of such dreams only fuelled his anger.

As the days plodded past, merging into the nights in one dark, meaningless trial of endurance, Robyn's anger became more focused. He concluded that the world was an evil, Godless place where the weak were tortured and exploited by those with power. There were no checks or balances. The law was a mere sham, a blunt instrument used and manipulated by the powerful to get what they wanted.

Robyn was a more than usually devout man. His anger curdled into cold, remorseless hatred as he thought of the Church, the great spiritual and temporal power, founded by Christ to provide a tangible link between man and God.

"The servants of God should be poor and humble," he shouted into the gloom, "and stand as a barrier between evil men and those who cannot defend themselves. Instead they have abandoned their charge and turned to the worship of Mammon."

His words echoed through the corridor outside, but met with no response save the occasional mocking snort from the gaoler or one of the guards.

"Fat, grasping, money-grubbing, whoring priests," he added for good measure, "every one of them has mortgaged his soul to the Devil. God curse all priests!"

"Save one," he muttered, thinking of his friend Brother Tuck, "one honest man among thousands."

It was a monk, Robyn remembered, who had betrayed him at Nottingham. A sallow-faced, spindle-shanked little bastard in the magpie robes of the Cistercians. Robyn pictured his face and fondly imagined smashing it to a pulp.

He knew he was uttering heresy. For that he could be burned alive, a far worse fate than the quick hanging which was already in store. He was past caring. When the guards came to take him for trial, he was resolved to attack them with his bare hands. They would be forced to kill him on the spot. Better a blade in the gut, and some degree of honour, than a length of hemp around the neck.

On the fourteenth or fifteenth evening of his captivity (he was losing track of time in that foul vault) the gate creaked open, and the gaoler entered with a companion.

Robyn had been drifting in and out of wakefulness. He looked up as light flooded into the dungeon, wincing at the pain in his eyes, and thought he must still be dreaming.

The gaoler's companion was Brother Tuck, tall and severe as ever, but dressed in the tunic and scapular of a Cistercian instead of his usual tattered brown habit. He stood like a statue beside the stunted gaoler, imperious as any Roman Emperor; his arms folded inside their long sleeves, and looked down his nose at the prisoners.

When his eyes met Robyn's, one of them closed for a fraction of a second in a wink. A warm glow of relief and joy washed through Robyn's tortured soul, and he had to exercise a great effort of will not to laugh.

"There he is," said the gaoler, pointing at Robyn, "but you won't get much sense out of him. He sits there all day, jabbering and shouting about priests. I think he's gone mad, to say the truth. This dungeon breaks men."

"God sifts us all, like grain from a sack," Tuck said in deliberate, pompous tones that were completely unlike him, "the good grain he keeps, and the bad is cast on fallow ground. This Robert Hode is one such bad seed."

The gaoler shifted uncomfortably. "As you say, brother," he replied, tugging his greasy forelock, "I've always been a good churchman myself. And I prays every night, regular."

"You talk to God? You think He is your friend?" asked Tuck, lifting his head slightly and fixing the smaller man with a disapproving stare.

"Yes…I…think so?" stammered the gaoler, cringing slightly as the monk's shadow loomed over him.

"Then you will be keen to make the Lord's acquaintance."

Even as he spoke, Tuck pulled his hands from their sleeves. A sliver of bright steel flashed in the darkness. It vanished as he thrust the knife into the gaoler's breast.

He clapped his free hand over his victim's mouth and drove him hard against the wall, holding him there until his muffled squeals and violent shudders had subsided. Then he carefully lowered the dead man to the ground, sawed through his belt and snatched the bundle of keys hanging from it.

"Tuck," said Robyn as the priest crossed over to him and started fiddling with the heavy padlock on the shackle fastened to his left wrist, "I scarcely hoped to - "

"Quiet," Tuck hissed, grimacing as he fought with the lock, "there is a guard on the door at the end of the corridor outside. He might hear us."

At last he found the right key, and with a grunt managed to twist it inside the padlock. The shackles sprang from Robyn's wrist. Gulping with excitement, he used his free hand to help Tuck with the remaining shackle.

Once he was free Robyn got stiffly to his feet, cursing the pains that shot through his cramped limbs. Tuck gave him a moment to stretch and massage his red-raw wrists.

"The guard," the priest whispered, "you stand by the door while I fetch him."

Robyn nodded. He looked around for a weapon and spotted a

dagger hanging from the dead gaoler's belt. He bent to retrieve the blade, slid it from its cheap leather sheath and soft-footed over to the doorway.

The other prisoners hadn't moved or made a sound while the gaoler was disposed of. Robyn glanced at them, wondering if they would be of any help. Both were staring at him, wide-eyed, but with little sign of wit or understanding on their haggard, grimy faces.

He put a finger to his lips. "Stay quiet, lads," he said. "You don't want any part in this."

Tuck hurried outside. "Guard," he cried, "come quick. One of the prisoners has been taken ill."

The sound of heavy footsteps echoed down the corridor. Robyn braced his back against the wall, dagger ready in his hand.

A heavy-set figure appeared in the archway. "Which one is it?" demanded a rough male voice, "I know these sods. They're always shamming."

Tuck had been careful to stay behind him. He wrapped one arm around the guard's neck and clamped a hand over his face. At the same time Robyn darted out of hiding and rammed his dagger up to the hilt in the guard's unprotected throat.

The guard wore a kettle hat, a kind of wide-brimmed helmet. It fell off as he jerked violently in his death-throes. Tuck made a grab for it, but it slipped through his fingers and landed on the flagstones with a loud, ringing clatter.

Tuck and Robyn stood frozen, holding the dying man upright between them as the echoes died away. It seemed to take an age. Robyn anxiously chewed his bottom lip, expecting any moment to hear the sound of raised voices and running feet as more guards came to investigate.

Nothing happened. The world beyond the doorway remained dark and silent. Exhaling, Robyn nodded at Tuck to help him put the dead man down. Cramp screamed in his arms and thighs as they lowered him gently to the ground.

"What now?" Robyn panted.

Tuck rose and beckoned him to follow. The priest's face was pale and set. Robyn could almost feel the tension radiating from him as they padded down the corridor and crept outside.

It was pitch dark outside. Robyn had no idea of the actual time, but guessed a couple of hours before midnight. The Inner Bailey was lit by torches mounted in brackets on the walls. More light streamed from the upper windows of the keep and a few of the outbuildings. The faint sound of music, pipes and a drum, drifted down from the hall on the first floor of the keep. There was no moon.

Robyn looked towards the squat drum towers of the gatehouse. Raucous voices spilled from a door set inside the gateway. Even in the poor light he could see that the portcullis was lowered.

Hope died inside him, but then Tuck seized his arm. Robyn allowed himself to be led towards a low arch in the wall flanking one of the corner towers of the keep.

The door stood open. They hurried through it and turned down a narrow, windowless corridor. Robyn could hear a babble of voices up ahead, and wondered why Tuck was heading towards them.

All became clear as the corridor opened out onto a small ground-floor chamber. A spiral staircase was visible beyond the door opposite. The stair led up to the hall and living quarters of the keep, where the voices came from, and down into the mysterious depths below the castle.

Tuck led him down. The stair was only wide enough for them to descend in single file. Robyn held onto the wall as he picked his way with care down the narrow, slippery steps.

He trusted in his friend's judgment. Tuck was not only the most intelligent man he knew, but the bravest, as tonight's work had proved.

The steps soon ran out and ended in a tunnel carved out of the sandstone by some long-dead workmen. It steadily narrowed as they descended further, until Robyn had to turn sideways to squeeze through. His feet slipped on the smooth floor. Old childhood terrors of being shut in enclosed spaces and buried alive resurfaced to clutch at him. He had to force himself to breathe deeply and ignore the pounding of his heart.

"How did you find this route?" asked Robyn in a hushed

voice, even though they were alone in the dark.

"I didn't," his friend replied, "I have never been down here before. Matilda bribed a man who works at the castle to show her where it ends, and tell her where the entrance in the keep was to be found. So you may thank your wife for your deliverance."

"And your courage," said Robyn. Tuck made no reply.

As they struggled on, Robyn kept his fear of enclosed spaces at bay by thinking about Matilda. During his time in the dungeon, in the small hours of the morning when his spirits were at their lowest ebb, he had often wept at the thought that he would never see her again.

Robyn felt as though God had plunged him into the furnace, but instead of destroying him the fires had cleansed his soul. His despair was lifted.

His anger remained. Robyn clenched his fist in the darkness, and swore a silent oath to devote the remainder of his time on earth to avenging the poor and downtrodden. It was a hopeless fight, for no man could take on all the powers of evil and hope to win, but someone had to make the gesture.

Even though, he thought with grim acceptance, *that man will be utterly destroyed.*

At last the tunnel started to widen out. Robyn felt a breath of wind on his face. He gloried in it, the first fresh air he had inhaled for weeks.

Tuck quickened his pace. "Almost there," he said, his voice cracking with excitement. Robyn stumbled over a small pile of bones, scattering them, but had no time to check if they were animal or human.

The cavern narrowed again to a final passage that sloped down to an opening. Robyn could see a face outside, silhouetted by the light of a torch, and cried out for joy when he recognised his wife.

"Matilda!" he shouted, his voice echoing and re-echoing through the twisting maze of tunnels under Nottingham Castle, and ran to meet her.

"No time," she said, laughing and almost dropping her torch as he swept her up in an embrace, "we must move quickly. Let me go, you fool!"

She pushed him off, though not before they had exchanged a lingering kiss. Tuck was already moving away to the right, keeping his back pressed against the rock.

"Douse that torch," he ordered, "we can't risk a light any longer than necessary."

Matilda had no means of dousing it, so she tossed it into the cave-mouth, where its flickering light was quickly swallowed up.

They followed the marshy riverbank that led away from the opening until they reached a thicket. Their horses were tethered to a couple of trees. Will was guarding the beasts, and grinned when he saw Robyn.

"You have the luck of the Saints," he said, pumping Robyn's hand, "or the Devil, I know not which."

Robyn's horse, a beautiful grey courser he had stolen from a Knight Templar, pawed the earth and neighed softly as she sensed him draw near.

"Good lass," he said softly, running his fingers through her mane, "missed me, have you?"

He untied the reins and climbed stiffly into the saddle. The prison cramps were almost too much to bear, and he had to bite back whimpers of pain as the others mounted and cantered away south, towards the hunting park next to the river.

The sense of freedom, of life regained and renewed, helped him forget the aches in his body. There was no sign of pursuit from the castle, looming grey and forbidding behind them on its great rock.

They rode at a fast canter, and were under the trees of the park before the sound of an alarm-bell echoed faintly behind them.

"Too late, my lord Sheriff," Robyn cried, urging his courser to the gallop, "far too late!"

The outlaws reached the safety of their camp in Sherwood without mishap. Littiljohn and the others were waiting to meet them, even though it was long past the hour when any sane men should have been in bed. They had caught a buck. The sight of the meat roasting on the spit warmed Robyn's soul, even as the delicious smell made his famished belly cramp with hunger.

His reunion with Littiljohn was awkward. They had quarrelled before Robyn left for Nottingham, and it would have been easy for him to blame the big man for his capture and imprisonment.

Fortunately, though impulsive and quick-tempered, Robyn was no fool.

"Tuck told me it was your idea to look for the tunnel under the castle," he said, offering Littiljohn his hand, "that means I owe you my life, at least in part. If I offended you, I apologise."

The rest of the band watched in tense silence, their faces illuminated by the glow of the fire. There was something vital about this reconciliation. Robyn was their acknowledged chief, but Littiljohn was a strong and persuasive character, and might have chosen this moment to challenge him for the leadership.

"No apology needed," grunted Littiljohn after a long moment, enfolding Robyn's hand in his own great hairy paw, "we were both fools. I am glad to see you safe."

That lifted the tension. "A toast!" shouted Will, springing to his feet and raising his cup, "to his lordship, the High Sheriff of Nottingham, for having the grace to let our master go free!"

Laughter rippled around the clearing, and a festival atmosphere settled over the camp for the remainder of the night and well into the morning. The outlaws sat or sprawled on the ground, eating their meat with bloody fingers and drinking stolen ale. All was good humour and fellowship, at least for the time being, and for a few hours they were able to forget the misery and cruelty of their lives.

5.

The outlaws laid low during the weeks immediately following the rescue of their chief. Robyn wished to take no further risks for a while, and was aware that the Sheriff would be enraged by the loss of his prisoner.

"If he has any pride at all, he will have troops scouring the countryside for me," he said, "John, what kind of man is this Fitz Nicholas?"

Littiljohn had served for a time in the Nottingham garrison. "I don't really know," Littiljohn replied with a shrug of his huge shoulders, "I only served under him for a few weeks. A practical man, I think, and like most Sheriffs inclined to feather his own nest. He will come looking for you, that is certain."

"After us," Matilda corrected him, "he will know that Robyn cannot possibly have slain two men and escaped on his own."

It was high summer, a time when men could live and sustain themselves in the forest. The weather was warm, even at night, and game plentiful. Robyn ordered his followers to keep to the deep forest, well away from the roads and highways that cut through the eastern and western fringes of Sherwood.

Even so, he occasionally posted scouts near the Great North Road. They brought back reports of mounted soldiers riding back and forth between Nottingham and York. Robyn supposed them to be carrying messages between the two High Sheriffs.

"They lack the manpower to besiege Sherwood," he assured Matilda, "the forest is over twenty miles wide and thirty miles long. Even if Fitz Nicholas makes things too hot for us here, we can always return to our old haunt in Barnsdale. They will never catch me again."

"Promise?" asked Matilda, huddling closer to him. It was late at night. They were lying under a shared wolfskin beside the dying embers of the fire. A half-moon hung in the velvet night sky, and all was peace.

"I promise on the Virgin," said Robyn, kissing her fingers. It was a solemn oath. He held the Virgin Mary in special regard.

At the same time it was a lie, uttered to give some measure of comfort to his wife. Something had happened to him in the darkness of his dungeon. A flame had been lit inside his soul, and only death could snuff it out. That death, likely to be a premature one, was as certain as snow in winter. The road he had chosen only ended one way.

Robyn took the first step on that road the following morning, when he gathered the outlaws around him after breakfast. Besides Robyn himself, their number was reduced to just ten. Tuck, who was in his late twenties but looked a couple of decades older, was by far the eldest.

The rest were frighteningly young. Their pale, guileless faces were full of the unquestioning hope and courage of youth. Robyn thought they looked like a pack of schoolboys as they sat cross-legged in a half-circle around him, waiting for him to speak.

He leaned against the trunk of the vast oak tree that dominated the clearing, and tried to order his thoughts.

"We are no common band of thieves," he said, "preying on the weak merely to survive. Any who wish to follow that path must leave now."

He paused, looking into each pair of eyes in turn. Simple trust and obedience gazed back at him.

I am leading them to their deaths, he thought, *and they will follow me without question.*

He hurried on before his will faltered. "These are my rules," he said, "and all who cleave to me must observe them. We will harm no husbandmen, that till with their ploughs. Nor any honest Christian knight, that behaves like a good fellow. We will be friends to those who suffer and spend their lives in toil, or feel the bite of the whip and the branding iron for breaking the forest laws to feed their families."

His voice rose as the rage boiled up inside him. "But these high churchmen, these bishops and archbishops and their ilk, these we shall beat and bind. These fatted clerics who feed off the blood and sweat of the poor, who abandon their vows to Christ for earthly gain, shall learn to give Sherwood a wide berth. No mercy for them, no pity! They have sinned, and their sins shall find them out!"

Robyn was shouting now, the passion flowing out of him. His followers responded. With the exception of Tuck and Matilda, they sprang to their feet and cheered, clenching their fists and echoing his war-cry.

"No mercy for churchmen! No pity! Their sins shall find them out!"

Even Littiljohn joined in, his deep-set eyes shining with a new respect as they fixed on Robyn. Any lingering doubts about Robyn's right to lead the outlaws were swept aside.

Robyn set out his plans. The outlaws would deliberately cultivate the friendship of the serfs living in the villages scattered about Sherwood, giving them presents of venison and stolen money in exchange for shelter from the elements and protection from the law when required. They would target travellers on the main highways that led through the forest, especially religious persons, for they were often the wealthiest and most deserving of being plundered.

"We shall not kill," he added, "except in dire necessity. Our aim is not to murder the rich, but humiliate them. None shall say we are just another gathering of cut-throats."

He noticed that Matilda and Tuck said little. Later, when the meeting had disbanded and the outlaws gone their separate ways until supper, they both reproached him.

Tuck was furious. "What was the meaning of that idiotic sermon?" he demanded, "you mean to wage war on the might of the Church, is that it? Some sort of inverted Crusade?"

Robyn faced him calmly. "If you like," he said, "though I can scarcely wage a Crusade with a dozen men. Someone needs to stand up to the greed and avarice of churchmen. They live in palaces and gorge on red meat, surrounded by treasures and soft furnishings, while the people they profess to serve live in poverty. Tell me, as a man of God, do you think that is right?"

"Of course I don't! Why do you think I left Fountains Abbey and joined the hermit of Knaresborough? I was cast out of Fountains for arguing with my brethren on just those points. Churchmen are supposed to be poor and humble, but they are not. The king and his barons are supposed to protect the people, but they do not. The world is full of injustice, Robyn. How much of injustice do you intend to fight?"

"As much as God allows."

He spoke with utter conviction. Tuck paused, searching his face. "Then you march freely to your own destruction," he said quietly.

Matilda's argument was simpler, and much more powerful. "I would not see you hang," she said, taking his hand, "you made a vow to me."

"I will keep it," Robyn replied, though his heart almost broke under the weight of another lie.

Nothing they said could dissuade him, and a few days later Robyn's faith in his cause received a boost.

It had been his custom in Barnsdale to levy a genial form of extortion on travellers, by inviting them to dine at his camp and then demanding payment for the meal. He decided to resurrect this custom in Sherwood, and posted men along the length of the Great North Road, waiting for some suitable person to invite to dinner.

Will and the one-eyed Thomas Alleyn returned to camp one golden afternoon, with dappled sunlight pouring through the canopy of the greenwood, and brought a guest with them.

He was a young man, fair-haired and pretty as an angel, though his good looks clashed with his ragged and stained clothing. He gave his name as Adam of the Dale, and his only possession of value was a battered old lute.

"I am a songbird," he declared when Robyn asked his trade, "fated to wander up and down the roads and byways of England, as my muse wills."

Robyn scratched his head and exchanged dubious glances with Matilda. "A minstrel, in other words," he said. "And not a very successful one, judging by your appearance. Times hard, are they?"

Adam coughed and had the grace to look embarrassed. "My art is not appreciated in high places. The barons spurn me from their households, forcing me to earn my pennies in low taverns and wine-shops. Clods. They would rather bellow along to dirges of Roland, and other such knightly oafs, rather than the glorious melodies I have to offer."

Robyn had to smile. "I like you," he said, "you won't compromise, even though it means poverty. You may eat with us, for no charge. I doubt you could pay anyway."

Adam's soft blue eyes lit up at the prospect of a meal. "My thanks, good outlaw," he cried, snatching up his lute, "as payment, in lieu of coin, let me sing for you."

Robyn was usually fond of music, but didn't want to listen to Adam's caterwauling while he ate. "What do you sing of?" he asked warily.

Adam gave him a cunning look. "Why, you, of course. You are Robyn Hode, are you not?"

"I am," Robyn said, surprised but gratified, "but how do you know me?"

"All the country hereabouts is alive with tales of your exploits. How you slew the dark knight, Sir Gui de Gisburne, and sent his headless body to York. How you escaped the wrath of the Sheriff of Yorkshire, fooled the King into sending a hundred men to look for you in the wrong place, and escaped the Sheriff of Nottingham's dungeons."

Adam plucked a simple melody. "You are Robyn Hode, the outlaw without peer," he sang in a low, tuneful voice, "the trickster who cannot be caught, the free spirit who thumbs his nose at the law."

Some of the outlaws laughed. Robyn was embarrassed. This description of his exploits was true, more or less, even if they were a combination of accident and luck.

"Enough," he protested, "I never heard such nonsense."

"Is that really what people are singing?" asked Matilda, "you have heard them?"

"Indeed, my lady," replied Adam with a graceful bow, "I set out from Carlisle a month ago, and since then have heard all manner of rhymes and verses about Robyn Hode. Poor stuff, mostly, composed by those who have not the skill for it. Many are mere thieves, and graft Robyn's name onto older tales."

"That is why," he went on, stroking out a chord, "I have chosen to compose true ballads of Robyn's adventures. No halfpenny rhymes, but a proper body of verse…with permission from the man himself, of course."

Robyn was at a loss. This ragged peacock was like no man he had ever encountered, completely unafraid at finding himself abducted by outlaws and spirited away into the forest.

He decided that Adam's girlish looks were deceiving. No man who journeyed through the turbulent, bandit-haunted north of England, on foot and alone, could be anything other than a tough and resourceful character.

"You are over-bold, fellow," he said sternly, "I don't take insolence from beggarly minstrels."

"Then slit my throat, if you have a mind," Adam replied carelessly, "let my blood run free into the soil from which it came, and release my soul into the heavens. The choir of angels shall acquire a fine new voice."

His absurd valour touched a chord in Robyn's heart. "No throat-slitting today, I think," he said, cracking a smile, "unless you insist on singing for your dinner. Sit at my right hand instead of Christ's, Adam of the Dale, and tell me something of your past. No doubt it is an interesting one."

Adam graciously accepted his invitation. He not only stayed for dinner, but the rest of the evening, and the next day, and the next, until Robyn grew used to his presence.

He could not only sing in a pleasant baritone that added a touch of gaiety to life in the forest, but shoot and fish and ride as well as any of the outlaws. His grace and courtesy were more suited to a great baronial household, and he was a surprisingly educated man, with a working knowledge of Latin and French. He could read and write almost as well as Tuck, who confessed to being delighted at the band's latest recruit.

"Someone of learning I can talk to," he said happily, "who has read a book or two, and is capable of discussing higher matters than hunting and the drinking of ale."

"I am beginning to think Adam is a nobleman's son," Robyn confided to Matilda, "banished for committing some offence or other, probably involving a woman. He seems far more cultured than most vagabond minstrels."

"You seem happy to keep him," said Matilda, "I think he appeals to your vanity."

"What do you mean?"

She fondly patted his cheek. "Don't sound so indignant, my love. There is a good deal of anger in you, and something of the play-actor as well. You want someone like Adam so he can compose ballads and tales of your deeds. Just as a troubadour sings the praises of the knights-errant he follows."

Robyn flushed, and hotly denied the charge of vanity, but only because his wife was right. She was learning to read him far too easily. What was the use of conducting a doomed war against oppression, if there was no-one to record it for posterity?

Thus Adam of the Dale was allowed to stay with the outlaws, and Robyn Hode acquired his first chronicler.

6.

Richard le Wys, vicar of the church of Applewick, hummed contentedly as he moved among the herbs and flowers of his walled garden. It was a glorious summer morning, and everything was blooming.

He had good cause to be content. True, he held the church of Applewick as a mere tenant for another clergyman, an Italian who preferred to stay in Milan and farm out his church and rectory to a native. Although an absentee, the Italian still benefited from the revenues, and part of Richard's job was to ensure that a good portion of the parish's income was diverted abroad.

So long as that was done, then Richard was left in peace to worship God, bully his servants and parishioners, and generally make himself comfortable.

The garden behind the rectory was his chief joy. He tended it as often as he could, but there were still a few weeds spotted about. Richard attacked them vigorously with his sickle. He would tolerate no blemishes here, his little private Eden.

He was on his knees, hacking away at a particularly stubborn root, when the sound of a door being flung open and running feet invaded his peace.

"Your Reverence," cried the voice of Matthew, the verger, "where are you, Your Reverence?"

Richard sighed, put down his sickle and struggled to his feet. He was carrying too much weight, and the effort made him puff.

"I'm here, Matthew," he said irritably, doffing the wide-brimmed hat he wore against the sun, "what is it? You know I don't like being disturbed in my garden."

Matthew halted, gaping and twisting his gnarled hands together like a nervous schoolboy in the presence of a master. He was an old man, lost somewhere in his mid-fifties, and had served the vicars of Applewick all his adult life. Despite this long term of service, he had never lost his air of cringing servility.

There were times when Richard rather enjoyed being fawned

31

over by this ridiculous little man. Today was not one of them.

"Well?" he demanded, stamping his foot, "don't stand there gawping like a landed fish. What is the matter?"

He had rarely seen Matthew so frightened. The old man's lugubrious face was drained of blood, and his entire body trembled.

"Something terrible, Your Reverence," he stammered, "something evil has appeared at the barns!"

Richard felt a twinge of anxiety. Matthew's fear was clearly genuine, and the thought of something terrible happening to the barns, or rather what they contained, was enough to bring the vicar out in a cold sweat.

The barns were three large storehouses on the western outskirts of Applewick, stuffed to bursting with sacks of grain held over from the previous harvest. The grain was destined, not to feed the local people who had harvested it, but to be carted off and sold for maximum profits in Nottingham market.

The absentee Milanese bishop expected a steady flow of income from his English diocese. It was Richard's duty to ensure the flow never ceased or faltered. If he failed (his duty towards God came a distant second) then the bishop would have him replaced. All the trappings of his pleasant existence - the garden, the pretty stone church, the comfortable rectory – would be whisked away and given to another.

He stuck out his heavy jaw and fixed Matthew with a fierce look. "Take a hold of yourself, man," he barked, "what is this nonsense you're babbling about? What evil?"

"You must come and see, Your Reverence. It is dreadful...unspeakable!"

There was plainly no sense to be got out of the verger, who looked on the verge of a seizure. Suppressing a blasphemy, Richard ordered Matthew to fetch his cloak.

The outskirts of the village were just half a mile away. Richard stalked angrily down the street, his cloak billowing behind him, ignoring the timorous greetings of the locals they encountered. Despite his obvious reluctance to return to the scene, Matthew was dragged along in the vicar's wake, whining and muttering prayers.

Soon they neared the storehouses, which were built on a piece of high ground overlooking the village. By now quite a crowd had gathered behind Richard, curious to see what their vicar was so annoyed about.

"There!" cried Matthew, "look there! God save us and protect us!"

He pointed a shaking finger at the single tree that stood on the summit of the ridge. It was an ancient beech, bowed with age and slightly crooked from centuries of being buffeted by high winds.

Richard's eyesight was poor, and he had to squint to make out the object dangling from one of the lower branches. An involuntary gasp escaped his lips when it came into focus.

The thing hanging from the tree had once been a man. Not just any man, but a Cistercian monk. His rotting body was garbed in the black and white robes of his order. They fluttered in the breeze, hiding the worst of their owner's decay from view. He had clearly been dead for weeks, judging from the ghastly greenish pallor of the shreds of flesh that still clung to his skull.

He was suspended from the branch via a length of rope tied about his neck. Richard's legs threatened to buckle under him as he gazed upon the horror. He almost vomited when a crow alighted on the dead man's skull and started pecking at the slimy remnant of his eye.

He swallowed the bile and made an effort to master himself. "Cut that thing down," he ordered, "this is all some foul trick. The culprits will be found and punished."

The peasant faces that looked back at him were rank with fear and superstition. "The Devil is here," whispered Wat the smith, a huge bear of a man reduced to a cowering child, "this is his handiwork."

"Don't be a fool," snapped Richard, but his own voice was shaking. Under his thin veneer of learning and pompous authority, he was as plagued with superstition as any serf. He came from base stock himself, and had clawed up the ladder to his present modest position through sheer drive rather than any great wisdom or piety.

A few of the villagers broke away and ran back to Applewick, crying that the Devil was loose.

"I'll not go near that tree," declared Martin, the reeve, "and nor will any who care for their souls. It is cursed. We are cursed. God has deserted us!"

Martin was a stolid character, not given to such outbursts, and his failure of nerve prompted the rest to surrender to panic. They took to their heels and scattered across the fields, Matthew among them.

Only Richard remained, rooted to the spot through sheer terror and a residual sense of duty. The dead man hanging from the tree had once been a fellow churchman. It was down to Richard to give him the last rites and a decent burial, whether or not the Devil lurked nearby.

The walk up the ridge was the longest of his life. He had never in his life been so scared. Stark winds howled across the bare, exposed ridge, while above his head ragged clouds scudded across a lowering sky. The clouds seemed to form and re-form into fell shapes, the cackling heads of demons and other hellish terrors, grinning down at the poor fool trudging to his doom.

Richard was still some distance from the tree when the high, piercing note of a hunting horn sounded somewhere to the east. He peered in that direction, his cloak whipping about him, and saw riders emerge from the trees, about quarter of a mile distant.

Applewick lay inside a clearing in the middle of the northern part of Sherwood. It was surrounded by deep forest, the home of devils and ogres and other such bogeymen.

Richard preferred not to think about the forest. At night his fearful mind often wandered through its darkest recesses, shivering at the nightmarish figures that lurked on the edge of sight and vanished when he tried to focus on them. The depths of England's forests belonged to an earlier age, before the light of Christianity arrived on these shores and drove out the false gods.

Or rather, drove them into hiding. The twelve hooded horsemen on the edge of the forest were straight out of one of Richard's nightmares. Faceless under hoods and masks, they looked scarcely human.

They spurred towards him, but he didn't run. There was

nowhere to run to. He had no weapon save the cross about his neck. His pudgy hand raised it high.

"Back!" he shouted, "get back, you envoys of Hell! Back to the pit you came from!"

It was a futile gesture. His voice was ripped away by the wind and had no affect on the riders. They galloped across the meadow at a tearing pace, led by a tall figure on a superb grey courser.

The horsemen surged up the slope and surrounded Richard, who collapsed to his knees and clasped his hands in prayer.

"Look at the man of God," said their leader, his voice slightly muffled and heavy with contempt, "do you call on Christ, Your Reverence? Do you expect him to descend from the heavens, with a host of angels at his back, to pluck you out of the mire?"

Richard glanced upwards. The man on the grey courser pushed back his hood, revealing a head of bristling reddish-brown hair and a pair of green eyes blazing with malice. The rest of his face was hidden by a scarf.

They were but men after all. Richard felt some relief at that. His spiritual terrors dissolved, but the earthly ones were still very much an issue. Every one of the hooded figures carried a sword and dagger.

He licked his dry lips, working up the courage to speak. "Robbers," he said, "murderers. Priest-killers. You will roast in Hell."

The red-haired man uttered a low chuckle and pointed at the dreadful corpse swinging in the wind. "You think we killed him, Your Reverence? Not so. God chose to snuff out his spark, though he deserved a worse death. His name was Brother William, and he betrayed me."

The name meant nothing to Richard. "Why are you here?" he demanded with a trace of his old asperity, "why did you hang up that poor man's body, instead of burying it like good Christians should?"

"Why, for your grain," the other replied, leaning over the pommel of his saddle. "Every last sack, or as many as we can carry. We hung up the corpse to frighten away your servants, thus sparing us a fight."

Richard stared up at him in horror. "Would you compound your sins and rob Christ? That grain belongs to the church!"

"Not so. It belongs to those who till and plant the earth. The grain will go to them, instead of being sold off in Nottingham at shameful prices."

The red-headed man drew his sword and levelled it at Richard. "We know all about your arrangement. You are paid a fat wage by the canons of York to milk the people of this parish for all they are worth, and send the profits to fill the coffers of some foreign bishop."

For a thief, he was remarkably well-informed. Richard could think of no ready retort, especially since it was all true.

"Go to the village," ordered the red-headed man, turning to two of his companions, "and fetch a wagon and horses. Pay the owners for their use."

Richard watched, helpless, as the two rode to the village. The others dismounted and led their beasts towards the storehouses.

He was left alone with their chief. "If you must steal from God," he said, "at least give the grain back to those who sowed and reaped it. The people of Applewick."

The green eyes above the scarf glinted with amusement. "How stupid do you think I am, Your Reverence? I know how you play the tyrant hereabouts, and how your least command is law to the serfs. If we gave them the grain, you would soon take it back again. No, it will be distributed among other villages, where the name of Richard le Wys is unknown."

Richard's fury and indignation overrode his fear. "Tell me your name, thief," he spat, "so I may curse it, bell, book and candle."

The horseman didn't respond for a moment. He was an imposing figure, tall and commanding as any lord, one fist planted on his hip.

"You will know my name soon enough," he said. "All of England north of Trent shall know it. For now, think of me as The Hooded Man."

7.

Robyn's strategy of attacking church property granted to absentee foreign clergymen proved a success. He did it to win popularity, for the farming out of English benefices to foreigners was deeply resented in the north by commoners and lords alike.

The grain stolen from Applewick was taken deep into Sherwood, and there stored in a hastily-built wooden shelter. Robyn had it divided up and taken out in equal amounts to the villages scattered about the forest.

"Should we give it all away?" asked Will, whose father was a cloth merchant, and had inherited the old man's eye for profit, "we could sell some off cheaper than the market price."

"And spend it on what?" Robyn replied with a shrug. "What we need to live, we take. The forest sustains us."

"For now, yes, in the summer months. Come the winter, and we might be grateful for having a pot of money put by."

Robyn could see the sense in that. Their funds had dwindled almost to nothing, thanks to the money spent by Matilda on bribing the Sheriff's cook, and of late the outlaws had robbed no-one on the highway. Robyn's new tactics, aimed at winning the love and support of the people, meant that their list of targets had narrowed.

"No," he said decisively, "we can't risk entering towns to sell the grain. By autumn we should have won enough friends to shelter us over the winter."

Will looked sceptical, but for the next few weeks all went according to plan. The free grain was received gratefully by the hobbled, black-gummed serfs of Clipstone, Worksop, Edwinstowe and other villages, whose brutish lives were one long struggle to stay alive. They were not used to charity, save the occasional scraps thrown to them by the Church, and their initial fear of the Hooded Man and his accomplices soon dissolved.

As the summer wore on, a golden time that Robyn would remember in future years with a sense of pride and regret, men started to come in from the villages to join the outlaws. Young men, mostly, bored of tilling the fields for their lords and yearning for some release from their lives of servitude and back-breaking labour.

"You must not encourage them," Matilda warned Robyn. "You risk turning honest men into outlaws like us and endangering their lives and freedom, to say nothing of their families."

"Every man follows his own path," he replied, "if these men want to fight instead of living as slaves, then I will not turn them away."

In deference to her wishes he took only the strongest of the volunteers, those who could hold their own with stave and dagger, and had some skill with the bow. They had to be strong of body and mind, not just to fight, but to stand a reasonable chance of surviving in the forest. The weather was still warm, and the game plentiful, but the scent of autumn was in the air.

"Sherwood is no place to be in the winter," remarked Littiljohn, "the snow lies thick, and the foresters freeze in their huts. We must find proper shelter before the cold draws in."

By the time the leaves started to turn brown, Robyn's band had swelled to over a score, almost as many as he had led in Barnsdale. Over half of the Barnsdale men were dead now, scattered and slain by the Sheriff's soldiers, but God had seen fit to give Robyn another opportunity. Robyn sensed that he was being tested, and vowed not to repeat his mistakes of old.

He was aided by the sheer size of Sherwood Forest, the largest royal forest in England, and a perfect haven for outlaws and broken men. It covered almost a quarter of Nottinghamshire, and contained woodland and heaths, chases and hunting parks, castles, towns and villages. The forest stretched into Derbyshire to the west, and its northern limits touched the borders of Yorkshire.

Parts of it were patrolled by royal foresters, employed by the king to guard his deer against poachers. Foresters were usually hard, competent men, used to being out in all weathers, and not easily intimidated. Robyn saw them as a problem, but fortunately their work did not include hunting down outlaws. So long as both parties kept their distance from each other, he reasoned, all would be well.

Then the unexpected happened. Three youths from Egmanton asked to join the band. Since they were big, capable-looking farm boys Robin permitted them to come to the outlaw camp for a trial.

First they were blindfolded, one of Robyn's precautions against treachery, and guided through the forest by Will and Littiljohn. When they arrived, and their blindfolds removed, the foremost went down on one knee before Robyn and presented him with a roll of parchment.

"A message from my lord, sir," the youth said nervously. "Sir Robert Deyville of Egmanton."

Frowning, Robyn studied the seal, which displayed a shield with a bar and a pattern of fleurs-de-lis. He knew of the Deyvilles, a knightly family who held several manors in Yorkshire as well as Egmanton.

"Here, Tuck," he said, passing the letter to the priest, "I read but slowly."

Tuck cracked open the seal and unfolded the parchment. "Sir Robert Deyville sends greetings to The Hooded Man," he read out, "and wishes him to know that Sir Robert sympathises with his crusade against the aliens. He sends these three men to serve in the crusade, and offers food and sanctuary to the outlaws if and when they should need it. If The Hooded Man is willing, Sir Robert would like to meet him on ground of his choosing on Lammas Day eve."

"He says nothing more," said Tuck, turning the parchment over, "save that it was signed and sealed at his castle of Egmanton, two days ago."

Robyn looked hard at the kneeling youth and his companions. "Why does your lord want to meet me?" he asked.

"I know not, sir," he replied, cringing slightly under Robyn's searching glare, "he bade me give you the message, but that was all."

The others also looked none the wiser. Robyn sent them off with Will for their trial, and turned to Tuck and Matilda.

"Well," he said, spreading his hands, "what do you make of

it?"

"It occurs to me," said Tuck, "that your legend has split in two. You are Robyn Hode, the arch-thief and trickster who laughs in the face of the law, and The Hooded Man, the mysterious robber who takes the Church's grain and gives it away for the benefit of the many."

"Judging from that letter," put in Matilda, "Sir Robert Deyville knows you as The Hooded Man, and approves of your fight against the influence of foreign priests. Perhaps he wants to help us."

"King Henry's decision to allow so many grants to papal servants in Italy was a terrible mistake," said Tuck, "it means that noblemen like Deyville are deprived of the money from church benefices on their lands. There is no surer way of making the barons fly to arms than threatening their profits."

Robyn stretched himself out on the ground. It was a roasting hot day, and the warmth seeped up from the ground into his bones.

"Knights and lords," he mused, scratching his beard, "other than old Fitzwarin, I never counted on their friendship. Unless it is a trap, and Deyville plans to clap me in chains and hand me over to the Sheriff."

"But he offers to meet on ground of your own choosing," Matilda reminded him, "and says nothing about how many men you can take."

"Where to meet him, though?"

"There is a cairn and an old stone cross near Blidworth," said Littiljohn, "piled up on the bones of some old Saxon prince, they say, who was killed in the forest while hunting. We could meet Deyville there."

Robyn concentrated, picturing the layout of the forest in his mind. He knew Sherwood reasonably well now, thanks to Littiljohn's knowledge and that of the local men who had recently joined the band. "Blidworth is a few miles south of Egmanton," he said, "and not a Deyville manor. He will have to leave his territory to meet us."

Littiljohn grinned into his beard. "Exactly."

Robyn called Deyville's messenger back. The boy returned,

sweating from his trial with the stave, and knelt before him.

"None of that," Robyn said irritably, gesturing at him to stand, "I'm not an earl, and don't require men to abase themselves before me."

"Listen," he went on as the boy rose, "you will go back to Egmanton, and tell your lord that I will meet him at Blidworth Cross on Lammas Day eve. He is to come accompanied by just one squire."

"Your pardon, sir," said the other, reddening, "but Sir Robert will not agree to that. He is a wary man, and will think you mean to take him for ransom."

Robyn pondered a moment. "Five men, then," he said, "but no more. If he attempts any treachery, it shall be met with steel. Tell him that."

Littiljohn blindfolded the boy, took him through the forest to the outskirts of his village, and released him with instructions to be there the next morning. He obeyed, and Littiljohn fetched him back with a verbal message from his master.

"Sir Robert agrees," he said. "My lord will meet you at Blidworth cross at sundown, with just five men at his back."

"Good work," replied Robyn, clapping him on the shoulder, "but you can stop referring to Sir Robert Deyville as your lord. You are part of my company now, and have no master but me."

Lammas Day was the first day of August, and the first harvest festival of the year. It was a time of old magic, when a loaf of bread made from the new wheat crop might be broken into four pieces and each piece placed in a corner of a barn, to protect the grain. It amused Robyn to imagine this pagan charm being observed by churchmen all over Nottinghamshire, desperate to protect their stores from The Hooded Man.

If so, the charm was destined to work, for he planned no robberies that day. He spent the morning arming his followers and telling them what was afoot. At noon Littiljohn led them towards the cross at Blidworth, which lay some eight miles from the camp.

The cross was a crudely-shaped piece of flint, weathered by time and mounted on a plinth beside the great pile of stones that formed the cairn. Long-dead hands had raised them in the centre of a little clearing, a silent and sinister place, haunted by old sins.

"There is no birdsong," observed Matilda with a shudder, "this place is tainted."

"The Saxon prince was murdered," said Littiljohn, "so the old story goes. Shot by one of his nobles as they chased a white hart through the forest."

"Like old William Rufus," remarked Tuck, "if only our ancestors had served more of the Norman kings in the same way, England might still be a free country."

Robyn looked at him with affection. There was real passion in the priest's voice. The outlaws were absorbing their master's anger, his determination to strike a blow against the tyrants that ruled their land.

There they waited for the remainder of the day. Robyn asked Adam of the Dale to lighten the grim atmosphere inside the clearing. The minstrel obliged, and plucked out some of his recent compositions, fragmentary tales of life in the greenwood in spring:

"In gentle May, when the woods are shining,
And the leaves are large and long,
It is pleasant in the fair forest,
To hear renewed birdsong,
To see the deer come to the dale,
And leave the high hills free,
And shadow themselves in the green fresh leaves,
Under the greenwood tree…"

His deep, pleasant voice had a soothing effect on Robyn's nerves. He smiled as the ballad went on to describe how Robyn tricked the Sheriff and slew forty-seven men in Saint Mary's church when they tried to take him.

"Forty-seven," remarked Tuck, resting his back against the cross, "I wonder that you needed my help to escape from that dungeon. You might have easily snapped your chains and killed the gaoler with your bare hands."

"Adam lies," Robyn said modestly, "it wasn't forty-seven. More like sixty."

At last the sun started to dip below the horizon, and the sky steadily darkened to a deep cobalt blue, glimmering with stars. The murmur of conversation among the outlaws ceased as darkness fell. Adam's lute played on for a while, playing a spare, melancholy air, but eventually even his music was smothered. The ancient stone cross was silhouetted in the gathering gloom, a gaunt reminder of fate and mortality.

Torch-lights flickered among the trees to the north. "They are coming," Robyn whispered to Matilda, "be ready."

His message was passed around the outlaws, who took up positions around the clearing. When Deyville and his men approached the cross, they would have a score of bows trained on them from all sides.

Robyn took a deep breath, pulled up his hood to hide his face, and stepped out alone. He walked slowly to the gap between the cairn and the cross, and stood there, waiting, thumbs tucked into his belt. He tried to look nonchalant, as though night-time conferences with powerful lords were nothing out of the way for The Hooded Man.

Six men emerged from the trees to the north. They walked in single file, leading their horses. Every man save their leader held a torch. Robyn recognised him by the arms on his surcoat as Sir Robert Deyville himself, a tall, sinewy man, about forty or thereabouts, hard-faced and with a touch of grey at the temples.

All six were armed for war, mailed and with broadswords strapped to their hips. Robyn didn't grudge them that, since only fools would venture unarmed to a meeting with a notorious outlaw, but something about Deyville's followers filled him with alarm. Every one wore a different set of arms on his surcoat, and carried himself with a certain arrogance and air of authority.

"Who are those men behind you?" he demanded, his voice sounding flat and lifeless in the dead night air, "they are no common soldiers or esquires."

Deyville halted at a respectable distance from the cross. "Nor are they," he replied in terse, clipped tones, "no more than five men, you said, and so I have obeyed. You said nothing about the identity of the five."

Robyn narrowed his eyes. He had to stay in control, and give no sign of panic or uncertainty. Deyville would sense that, like a wolf scenting blood. "Name them," he snapped.

"Certainly." Deyville gestured at his companions to step forward. They were all much alike, grim, hard-looking men, with a hawkish Norman cast to their features.

"Sir Peter de Brus," he said, indicating each man in turn, "Sir Peter de Mauley, Sir William de Percy, Sir Richard de Riparia, Sir Robert de Ros."

Robyn swallowed. This was a roll-call of northern barons. Not quite in the uppermost tier, true, but formidable enough. He recognised the stocky, red-haired figure of Percy, who had once been his lord before Robyn shot Sir Gui de Gisburne and fled into outlawry.

Fortunately, Percy couldn't recognise him under his hood. "Why did you ask to meet me?" Robyn asked. "And why have you brought these men with you? I have nothing to say to the lords of this realm. My concern is for their victims."

He recalled one of the miserable, hopeless wretches he had shared a dungeon with. "That one," he added, pointing at Sir Peter de Mauley, "is a liar, and a greater thief than I could ever be. He persecuted a poor miller and stole his land."

Mauley's coarse face flooded with angry blood, and his hand went to his sword. "Peace," said Deyville, stepping between them, "we have come to parley, not to fight. Whatever the differences between us, we share a common enemy. Those foreign priests whom the King has granted so much church land and revenue."

"We are opposed to them for different reasons," said Robyn, keeping his eye on Mauley, "I seek to give back what they steal to the poor. You have been hit in your purses, and seek revenge."

Deyville spread his hands. "What does it matter? We have pleaded to King Henry for redress, but like his father he refuses to listen. Thus we turn to The Hooded Man for aid."

Robyn said nothing for a moment. His mind raced. Silence reigned in the haunted clearing. The stone cross seemed to loom larger than ever.

"You would ally with me," he said eventually, "and help me fight the corruption of the church?"

Deyville coughed. "Not the church, as such," he said, looking uncomfortable, "but those who serve the foreigners. They are our enemies. We would not risk permanent excommunication."

Robyn grinned. "What does it matter?" he asked.

8.

Eustace of Lowdham travelled to Nottingham with a strong escort of five knights and their esquires and twenty mounted crossbowmen. The roads through Sherwood, as his colleague Fitz Nicholas had warned in his letter, were not safe.

"The more inaccessible parts of the forest are entirely given over to the rule of an outlaw known as The Hooded Man," the letter read, "I can do nothing with him. The local villagers refuse to yield up his whereabouts, and I dare not send men into the forest looking for him. They would come back bootless, or not at all. I suspect that the Hooded Man is none other than Robert Hode, who has been the cause of many of our trials of late…"

Eustace groaned when he read this. He might have known that Fitz Nicholas would make a botch of a simple execution.

"Blasted oaf," Eustace snarled to his wife, "and now he wants me to heave my guts down to Nottingham, doubtless to enlist my help in catching this bloody outlaw."

"I can't imagine why," Isabel replied tartly, "it's not as if you have enjoyed any more success. By rights, this Robert Hode should have been swinging from your gallows months ago."

In the end, Eustace was grateful to get out of York for a while, away from the constant sniping of his wife and the strain of keeping order in a large county with few resources. He left his capable Breton, Alan, in charge of the depleted garrison, with orders to do nothing foolish while he was absent.

The journey to Nottingham was uneventful, though Eustace's nerves were scraped raw by the time the city gates came in sight. He had ridden through Sherwood in a state of nervous paranoia, constantly scanning the trees for any sign of movement. The forest was peaceful and silent, which only added to his fears.

Fitz Nicholas greeted him at the gate with a show of bonhomie, though Eustace detected signs of stress: the Sheriff of Nottingham was a big, heavily-built man, but had definitely lost weight. The skin of his bulldog face hung in loose folds, and the tendons of his thick neck were prominent. His complexion was sallow, his eyes tired, and there was a strong hint of wine on his breath as he folded Eustace in a rather too tight embrace.

They rode through the marketplace to the castle, talking of inconsequential matters. Eustace noted a sullen, resentful look to the citizens, and felt their malicious glares boring into his back. Royal officials were never popular, especially those responsible for enforcing the law and collecting tax, but this level of hostility was unusual.

His suspicions were confirmed by the double guard Fitz Nicholas had posted on the castle gates, and the crossbowmen on the rampart.

"What has happened, Ralph?" he asked as the portcullis slammed down behind them, "why the extra guards?"

Fitz Nicholas passed a shuddering hand over his face.

"Not here," he muttered, glancing significantly at the soldiers and attendants all around them, "we must speak in private."

Baffled, Eustace gave his horse to a groom and followed his colleague across the inner ward, to the wooden steps leading up to the first floor of the keep.

Fitz Nicholas said nothing more until they had mounted the spiral stair leading to his quarters on the upper floor. There he ushered Nicholas into a room that served as bedchamber and study, and bade him take one of the benches by the fire.

Eustace waited impatiently while the other man poured two enormous measures of strong Gascon wine and handed him a cup. Fitz Nicholas's hand, he noticed, still trembled.

"Your letter informed me that the Hooded Man is in Sherwood," he said, taking a tentative sip, "and had taken control of large stretches of the forest. It seems his influence has spread into the city. In God's name, Ralph, what are you doing? Extra guards on the walls, the portcullis lowered during daylight? The outlaws will smell your fear."

Fitz Nicholas took a hefty gulp of wine and stared into the fire. The tawny flames were reflected in his heavy, red-rimmed eyes. Tiny hellfires danced in the depths of his irises.

"If it was just The Hooded Man I had to worry about," he said slowly, "all would be well. A few ragged outlaws, no matter how clever and popular, are only a limited threat by themselves."

He leaned forward and tapped Eustace's knee. "He is acquiring allies, Eustace. Powerful allies. My agents have seen The Hooded Man and his followers riding from castle to castle. Local knights are giving them shelter. The number of his followers has swelled recently, and raids on church property have multiplied. His allies are not only giving him shelter and protection, but men. Soldiers."

Eustace sniffed. "You have cause for concern," he admitted, "but this is nothing new. I recall a few years back, when I was deputy Sheriff in Yorkshire, a murderer named John de Thornton made friends with certain local knights. They gave him a roof over his head and enough cloth to fit out his men in green livery. We still caught the bastard, and hanged him high."

Fitz Nicholas put down his cup, rubbed his cheeks, picked it up again, and suddenly rose from his seat. There was something agitated about him, as though he had more to say, but couldn't bring himself to speak.

"What is it, Ralph?" Eustace demanded.

His colleague lumbered to the other side of the room and gazed forlornly out of the pair of arched windows.

"The King is furious," he said, "at our failure to catch Robert Hode, and the expense of sending a hundred mercenaries to York, when all the while the outlaw was in Nottingham. I mentioned that I suspect Hode and The Hooded Man to be one and the same. Too much of a coincidence."

"I don't believe in coincidences," said Eustace, "but there is much in what you say. So the king is angry. We both faced his father in a rage, and came off none the worse. What else?"

"Some weeks ago, King Henry received a message from a papal envoy. His Holiness has heard of the robberies and outrages committed on church property and servants in England. He ordered Henry to deal with the matter, or lose the friendship of the Vatican."

Eustace gave a low whistle. Such a threat was enough to sting Henry into action. Like his father, he relied heavily on papal support, and had allowed the numerous grants to Italian clergymen in order to win the Pope's favour.

"It seems our little outlaw has caused quite a stir," he said, "that's all to the good. Perhaps Henry will finally realise that keeping his Sheriffs on a meagre budget is no way to maintain order."

Fitz Nicholas turned to face him. "There is more. His Holiness evidently doesn't trust the King of England to carry out the task. So far as Pope Gregory is concerned, the Hooded Man is not just an outlaw, but a heretic. His Holiness is apparently setting up a papal inquisition, to root out heresy wherever it may be found."

"He means to test it on England," said Eustace.

"Yes. The envoy he sent to England was no ordinary papal messenger, but a Franciscan priest named Odo de Sablé. Odo is a protégé of Konrad of Marburg."

A cold finger of dread slid up Eustace's spine. Konrad of Marburg was already notorious across Europe. The Pope had sent him to suppress the Albigensian heretics in Germany and France. Lurid stories had filtered to England of the burnings and massacres Von Marburg carried out in the name of God.

"Odo arrived in London with a retinue of Templar knights," Fitz Nicholas went on, "eight Hospitallers and their esquires, and a strong force of sergeants and crossbowmen. The King greeted him with all humility and agreed to his every demand."

Eustace waited, fearing the worst. "Odo demanded the right to hunt The Hooded Man in person, and to employ whatever methods he thought best. The King agreed, and now Odo and his Templars are already on their way to Nottingham. The royal envoy publicly announced their coming in the market-place. Damned idiot. That is why the people look so resentful. They are terrified of what might happen, and blame me for it."

"No," Eustace said hoarsely, "there will be no burnings here. This filthy priest can demand what he likes in London. He has no authority north of Trent."

"He has the authority of King and Pope behind him. There is nothing we can do save comply."

Eustace stood up. "I am going back to York," he said, snatching up his cloak, "if de Sablé so much as sets foot in my jurisdiction, I will throw him into the sea."

Fitz Nicholas caught his arm. "Eustace, don't be a fool. He is coming north with over two hundred men at his back, including the Hospitallers and some royal troops. Even together, we don't have the strength to resist him. Nor can we disobey the King."

"You disappoint me. I never thought you a coward."

To Eustace's surprise, this had no effect. The Sheriff of Nottingham was a proud man, but something about the imminent arrival of a papal inquisitor had unmanned him.

He could hardly blame Fitz Nicholas for being perturbed. This Odo de Sablé was vested with the supreme authority of the pontiff in Rome, and had learned his trade from the notoriously cruel and bloodthirsty Konrad von Marburg. He was a formidable prospect.

"What, then?" asked Eustace, pulling his arm away, "you could have told me all this in your letter. Why have you dragged me down here?"

"I thought that together we might impress him with a show of strength. Demonstrate that we are not to be bullied. I could not say as much in the letter. It might fall into the wrong hands and compromise me."

Eustace looked doubtfully at his colleague. Judging from appearances, Fitz Nicholas was a broken reed, and de Sablé hadn't even arrived yet.

"When do you expect him?" he asked.

"Sometime tomorrow. He should be here already, but is moving slowly."

"Of course he is. A stately progress north, to impress the stupid English with the power and majesty of the Pope."

He thought for a moment. "I will stay," he said finally, "perhaps you are right. Together we might be able to restrain this damned Franciscan from lighting too many candles."

And I can pour some courage into you, he added silently, reaching for the wine jug.

As Fitz Nicholas predicted, Odo de Sablé reached Nottingham the next day. The sentries on the city gates spotted his entourage just before noon, which gave the two Sheriffs time to compose themselves. Fitz Nicholas had a sore head, thanks to Eustace's over-zealous efforts to drown his fear in drink the previous night, and was in a liverish mood.

"I propose we let him come to us," said Eustace as they conferred in the Great Hall, "and receive him here instead of waiting at the city gate. Give him a cold welcome."

Fitz Nicholas grimaced and pressed a cloth soaked in water to his brow. All around them was noise and feverish activity as the servants hurriedly cleared away the remains of breakfast. Fitz Nicholas's anxiety had affected his household, and an atmosphere of fear and uncertainty had settled over the castle. Even the dogs slunk about with their heads bowed and tails tucked between their legs.

"I agree we shouldn't fawn over him," he muttered, "but let's not alienate the man. Greet him politely, feed and house him and his soldiers, and wish them good hunting. With luck, Robert Hode will lead them in circles around Sherwood until they drop dead of exhaustion."

Eustace grinned. "Not two days ago we were desperate to hang Hode. Now we rely on him to deal with a greater enemy. God has a rare wit sometimes."

In the event, Fitz Nicholas rode out with six knights to greet the inquisitor at the gate, while Eustace stayed behind. He climbed the stair to the roof of the keep and watched from the battlements as the inquisitor and his entourage entered Nottingham.

De Sablé was clearly visible at the head of the procession as it rode through the market square. Fitz Nicholas rode at his right hand, looking pale and diminished. The Hospitallers were next, distinctive in their black cloaks stitched with white crosses at the shoulder. Sunlight glinted off their helms, and the spear-heads of the squires and sergeants that rode two abreast behind them.

Eustace had pictured the inquisitor to be a tall, imposing figure, lean and cadaverous as such fanatics tended to be. In fact he was rather short and stocky, and rode with an easy, relaxed posture, smiling and nodding amiably at the few citizens gathered to witness his arrival. He wore the loose brown habit of a Franciscan, belted at the waist, and there was nothing particularly grand or self-important about his appearance. It was difficult to be sure at such a distance, but he seemed to be in plump middle age, pink-cheeked and agreeable rather than handsome. The sort of man one's eyes quickly got bored of looking at.

The market square was usually bustling, but today most people had stayed at home, fearful of this angel of death that the Pope had sent among them. A strange, unnatural silence had fallen over the city, broken only by the tolling of the bell in Saint Mary's Church and the ominous plainchant of the monks. They had gathered to sing in the inquisitor's honour, no doubt hoping to impress him with their devotion.

Eustace shook his head. If de Sablé proved as bad as he feared, and demanded the burning of so-called heretics, it was clear the local clergy would do nothing to oppose him. Rather, they would applaud his monstrous judgments, and help him light the pyres.

He nerved himself to face the coming trial, and slowly descended to the Great Hall.

9.

Matilda insisted on going to Applewick to spy on the Franciscan and his followers, even though Robyn forbade and finally pleaded with her not to take the risk.

"Because I am your wife, and you couldn't bear to lose me?" she retorted, "or because I am the only woman here, not fit to share the dangers of the men?"

Robyn looked at her despairingly. "Perhaps a little of both," he admitted. "There is no question of your worth. If not for you, I would be still rotting in the Sheriff's dungeon, or more likely dangling from a cage in Nottingham market."

"I want to see what this foreign priest is doing," she said stubbornly, "you would be happy to send any of the others, so why not me?"

"I am reluctant to send anyone. Thomas tells me the Franciscan has eight Hospitallers and another twenty or thirty soldiers with him. We must keep our distance."

"One or two scouts won't be in much danger. We can see the village from the edge of the forest. They won't spot us."

Her husband considered. "I will go with you," he said finally, "and see you safe."

"Please," she pleaded, "don't nursemaid me. I do want to prove my worth. I want to show that I am more than just your consort."

"Will can go with you," Robyn said firmly, "and that is my last word on the matter. Take my courser. If you are pursued, she will carry you out of danger."

Delighted, Matilda kissed him, and promised to be back by sundown. "Keep to your vow," he murmured, holding her close, "as I keep to mine."

She took the courser, a pliant beast that offered no objections to the unfamiliar weight on her back, and rode out with Will.

Applewick was over an hour's ride away. They made their way cautiously through the woods, following familiar paths until they reached the highway that cut through the eastern part of Sherwood.

The way to Applewick lay along a rutted side-road that branched off the highway, leading north-west into the depths of the forest. It was another hot, dry day in early autumn, but the road was churned up by the passage of over thirty sets of hoofs.

"Thomas tracked them this far," said Will, "but turned back when he saw them taking the Applewick road. There is nothing at the end save the village."

Applewick was the first village the outlaws had raided, as part of Robyn's new strategy of targeting the church.

The mysterious Franciscan had crossed the Trent four days ago, accompanied by an impressive entourage of knights and sergeants. Robyn's informants among the villages south of Nottingham had told him as much, and that the newcomer had been entertained for two nights at the castle. Both the Sheriffs of Nottingham and Yorkshire were present, suggesting they held the Franciscan in a high degree of fear or respect.

Now he had set out from Nottingham with part of his following, and descended upon a humble village deep inside Sherwood. Matilda's lively imagination whirled as she tried to fathom his reasons.

"Best to lead our horses on foot," said Will, sliding nimbly from his saddle, "keep them fresh, in case we are ambushed on the way."

She followed his example. Together they proceeded cautiously along the road, in places little more than a bumpy track. Judging from their footprints, the soldiers had also been obliged to dismount, and made their way in double or single file.

The track opened out onto the patchwork of fields that surrounded the village. Before they reached that point, Matilda and Will tethered their horses and crept through the undergrowth towards the edge of the trees.

Applewick was made up of fourteen or longhouses and smaller huts arranged in a loose circle around the church, a pretty stone building dating from before the Conquest. The rectory, where the local vicar resided, was at the northern end of the village, while some rising ground to the west was occupied by the storehouses the outlaws had plundered.

Matilda's eye was drawn to the fields south of Applewick.

The barley crops had been reaped and stored, leaving a wide expanse of bare brown soil.

The villagers, some fifty people, were gathered in a ring around a great pile of timber and brushwood. Sixteen crossbowmen in white cloaks and tunics sat their horses nearby. Their weapons were loaded and trained on the crowd.

Inside the ring was the Franciscan on his roan mare, protected by eight Hospitallers. Matilda had never seen these famous warrior-monks before, and drew in a sharp intake of breath at the sight of their black cloaks and gleaming mail. Two of the knights were dismounted, and held burning torches.

"Oh Christ," breathed Will, "the poor wretch."

He referred to the iron stake, some eight feet high, thrusting up through the middle of the heap of timber. Tied to the stake was a thin young man, clad only in his night-shirt. Matilda recognised him as John Maker, one of those who had volunteered to join the outlaws, but was turned away for not being skilled enough with bow and stave.

Matilda's skin crawled at the certain knowledge of what was going to happen to him. She had heard rumours of people being burned alive in distant Germany and France, where the church was always busy suppressing heretics, but never imagined such horrors could occur in England.

The Franciscan was in the midst of a speech. He was a short, burly man, but had a voice like a war-horn. Its strident tone echoed across the flat fields and reached the outlaws in their hiding place.

"You have all benefited from the actions of heretics," he boomed, "and thus stand condemned of heresy yourselves. No trial is necessary. The Devil came bearing gifts, and like good Christians you should have refused them. Instead you fed off grain belonging to holy mother church."

He flung out an arm and pointed to the boy tied to the stake, weeping and struggling in vain against his bonds. Matilda recalled he had no family, his parents and sister having been carried off by plague the previous winter. An easy target.

"This one has consorted openly with the heretics in Sherwood!" the Franciscan went on, "he flirted with the Devil and offered to join the ranks of the damned. For that, he will burn."

That was the signal for his Hospitallers to thrust their torches into the pyre. The wood was tinder-dry, coated with pig's grease, and the flames quickly took hold.

A great wail went up from the villagers. Some of them pressed forward. The Hospitallers blocked their way with drawn swords.

"For every day that Robyn Hode remains free," bawled the Franciscan, raising his voice above the crackle of flames and the shouts of the crowd, "I will condemn one of you to the fire. You know where he hides in Sherwood. Betray him. Bring him to me. Or burn!"

"Come away," said Will, touching Matilda's arm, "we shouldn't watch this."

"We can't just run away and leave that poor devil to burn!" she cried, even though she knew it was hopeless. There was nothing they could do to save John. The flames had already reached his legs. His shrieks of agony and terror drifted across the fields, accompanied by the rank stench of burning flesh.

"Back to the camp," he said, "Robyn must know of this."

He rose and scrambled away through the undergrowth. Matilda followed like one in a dream, striving to block out the horror of what was happening behind her.

10.

When he heard of the burning at Applewick, and the Francisan's threat, Robyn made no quick decisions. Instead he sought the solitude of a grove a little way from the camp, where he could pray and beg for guidance from the Virgin.

The grove was his private refuge, a small clearing in the woods with a narrow stream running through the middle. Deprived of a church, Robyn found this peaceful spot the nearest thing to a place of worship.

He spent the best part of an hour here, sitting by the stream and gazing into the crystal-clear waters. A tall, sinewy man with startling green eyes and a shaggy growth of reddish-brown hair and beard gazed back at him. Robyn's face had aged in recent months. He had acquired a gaunt, hunted look, hardly surprising considering the trials and dangers he had endured.

It was a bitter thing, he reflected, that all his adventures had led him to this. He had come to accept that he was destined for a bad end, but not so soon. There were so many things left to be said and done.

"I am not prepared," he said aloud, "I don't want to go."

The admission of weakness brought tears to his eyes. Robyn wiped them away and knelt in prayer by the water. He mouthed silent words, humble pleas to the Virgin, asking her to watch over his loved ones after he was gone.

When he was done, and his mind settled, he got up and returned to the camp. There he summoned the outlaws to a meeting around the Major Oak where he had first addressed them.

Their numbers had continued to swell in recent weeks. Robyn now had a following of thirty-four men (and one woman). They were a hard and capable set now, sharpened by the rough life of the forest, hunting, and constant practice with weapons.

Even so, Robyn still despaired at their youth, and the devoted loyalty he seemed to inspire. He had given these peasant boys an alternative to the hard and unforgiving lives they were born to endure. More than that, he had given them a cause. Robyn looked at their earnest, trusting faces and wondered if he not committed some grave sin by doing so.

"Have you told them?" he asked Matilda. She nodded, white-faced, her eyes haunted by the atrocity they had witnessed.

"This Franciscan priest, whoever he might be," said Robyn, turning to the outlaws, "has threatened to murder the people of Applewick unless they betray me. That they cannot do, for none of them know the whereabouts of our camp."

He paused, struggling to appear calm despite the emotions raging in his breast. "I won't let innocents die for my sake," he went on, "and will have no more unnecessary deaths on my conscience. I have prayed, and decided to hand myself over to the Franciscan. Today. Now."

Robyn had steeled himself for the consternation that followed, but was taken aback by the force of it. As one his followers rose and clustered around him, shouting denials and swearing that they would not allow him to go.

"Lads," he cried, almost laughing as he held out his hands to press them back, "there is no help for it. We cannot fight the priest. He has armed knights and soldiers at his command. Hospitallers, God help us!"

"Fuck them," said Littiljohn, succinctly expressing the general opinion, "and to hell with the Franciscan. I will see him burn him on his own pyre before he lays hands on you."

Other voices joined in. "You will not go," said Matilda, sliding her hand into Robyn's, "remember your vow to me."

Hers proved the most persuasive voice of all. Robyn was almost overcome with sadness as he looked at her. His vow was a lie, and God was making him pay for it.

"If you won't let me give myself up," he said when the clamour had died down, "then we must fight. Matilda, how many men did you say he had?"

"Eight Hospitallers," she replied, "and sixteen crossbowmen."

Robyn thought quickly. Twenty-four men, eight of them among the most elite warriors in Christendom, all armed and mounted. The outlaws, with their bows and staves and complete lack of armour, would be slaughtered in a straight fight.

"Don't forget the villagers," said Tuck, "if they see us attack, they may join in. The Franciscan committed a foolish error by killing one of them. He should have made the threat, but not carried it out. Now he has earned their hatred in place of fear."

Robyn clutched his head. Thirty-odd ragged outlaws and fifty peasants against trained soldiers. For a moment he considered dropping the idea. Memories of his defeat in Barnsdale were still painful, and the faces of his dead followers haunted his dreams. He had failed them. Now he was destined to fail again.

There was no escape. Even if he tried to deliver himself up for judgment, the outlaws would not let him go. He had no doubt that Littiljohn would physically prevent him. The giant loomed over Robyn, beard bristling, brawny arms folded across his massive chest.

"Well, then," said Robyn, smiling weakly at his men, "it seems I have brought you to the ring. You must dance if you can."

The outlaws moved like wolves through Sherwood at night, guided by their knowledge of the forest and the silvery light of a half-moon. They had set out at midnight. Robyn's aim was to reach Applewick in the early hours of the morning, when most men were at their lowest ebb, and fall on the Franciscan's troops while they were still mazed with sleep.

He expected the priest to have posted guards, and so the outlaws slowed their pace when they drew closer to the village. They had bypassed the road, it being the most obvious approach, and cut directly through the woods instead.

Rain whispered through the trees as they loped through the undergrowth, sure-footed as any wild beasts. Robyn was in the forefront, but Matilda was fastest of all. She bounded along a few paces in front of him like a young deer. He had briefly considered ordering her to stay behind, but one look at her face persuaded him otherwise.

Their pace slowed to a crawl when the lights of the village glimmered through the trees. Robyn passed the word for Will and Tuck to join him, and crept forward with just them for company. They moved swiftly and quietly, daggers gripped tightly in their fists.

"Curse Littiljohn," muttered Will, "he runs with the grace of an ox. You can hear his breathing for miles."

Robyn grinned in the darkness. They were right at the edge of the trees now. He sat on his haunches and peered at the village. The lights came from the rectory and the church. All the other buildings were dark and silent. There was a fire lit on the hill where the store-houses stood. The Franciscan had posted men there to keep watch through the night.

Robyn ground his teeth when he saw the pyre. It still smouldered, and the blackened remains of the Franciscan's victim were still tied to the stake. He remembered John Maker, a lively youth, somewhat dull-witted and weak of body, but pleasant and honest, and undeserving of such a horrific fate.

Guilt stabbed at him. If he had not turned John away, the boy might still be alive. The only consolation was that some other innocent would have been sacrificed to lure him out of Sherwood.

"Your eyes are better than mine," he whispered to Will, "I count three men on that hill. What can you see?"

Will rose on the balls of his feet and squinted at the hill. Silhouetted in the moonlight slanting through the trees, his bony frame took on the appearance of a cadaver. Robyn was put in mind of the corpse of Brother William, and how the outlaws had hung it from the tree overlooking Applewick. The dead Cistercian's remains no longer dangled from the branch. The vicar must have ordered them taken down and given proper burial.

"Yes, three men," said Will, "the firelight catches their helms. There may be more in the barns, though."

"We will have to take the risk," said Robyn, "Tuck, take word back to Littiljohn. He is in charge now. If he sees the fire go out, he is to lead the men onto the hill. If we have not returned by dawn, he will take them back to camp."

"Matilda is to go with them," he added as Tuck moved away, "that is an order."

Tuck soon returned, and together the three men left the shelter of the trees and padded towards the hill. They removed their shoes, for ease of movement and so their approach would go unheard by the men on the summit.

They dropped to all fours and swarmed up the slope, hoods raised and daggers clenched between their teeth. As they neared the ridge, Robyn laid flat on the grass and gestured at the others to do the same.

For a few seconds they lay quiet, listening to the low murmur of voices from above. The soldiers were speaking in Italian, but Robyn recognised the sound of tired, bored men who would much rather be asleep in the warm.

Tired, bored, and off-guard. Or so he hoped.

Robyn removed the dagger from his mouth and squirmed forward a few inches until he could see over the crest.

He saw three men garbed all in white, with black crosses sewn onto their cloaks at the shoulder. For one heart-pounding moment he thought they were Hospitallers, but then saw the crossbows stacked on the ground beside their fire.

They had found a bench from somewhere. Two of the men were seated on it with their backs to him. The third stood and used a long spoon to poke the contents of an iron pot hanging from a spit over the fire. Rain drizzled among the flames, causing them to flicker and spit.

The soldiers looked hard, capable sorts, more than a match for the outlaws in a fair fight. Robyn's best chance was to catch them unawares and make the advantage count.

He crawled back down the slope. "Three men," he whispered, "two with their backs to us. Will, take the one on the left, Tuck the right. Swift and quiet."

They didn't need telling. Will was the most skilled knife-man in Robyn's following, and he had witnessed Tuck despatch two men in Nottingham's dungeons with terrifying efficiency.

Robyn left himself with the responsibility of dealing with the third man. He pictured the distance between them and the fire. Roughly ten to fifteen paces. They would have to be quick.

He took a deep breath and launched himself over the ridge. Tuck and Will sprinted to his left. The steel of their daggers glinted in the moonlight.

They were on the soldiers before the latter knew what was happening. Tuck and Will seized their targets by the neck.

Blades slashed for exposed throats.

Robyn's attention was fixed on his man. He had dropped his ladle as he saw the shadows springing out of the night, and clapped a hand to the knife at his belt. His mouth opened to shout a warning.

The fire lay between them. Robyn leaped over it, scattering ash and pieces of burning timber, and dived. His shoulder connected sharply under the soldier's ribs and knocked the breath out of him. They fell in a heap, Robyn on top, stabbing wildly. The soldier got his left arm up, shielding his face, and tried to draw his knife with his right hand.

Robyn's free hand gripped the soldier's throat and squeezed. The flow of Italian curses was cut off. Robyn tried to follow up by driving his knee into the other's crotch. He missed, but the Italian's left arm slackened as the latter fought for breath. Robyn pressed down with all his weight, gasped as something cut into his hip, and stuck his knife into the soldier's left eye.

His hand was still on his victim's throat. The dying man jerked and shuddered violently under him, blood spurting from his punctured eyeball. Robyn rammed the blade in further until it pierced the brain. The soldier gave one final heave, and then went still.

Panting, Robyn wiped the spots of blood from his face and sat up. He saw that Will had disposed of his man neatly enough, but Tuck was in difficulty. His target had got a hand to Tuck's wrist as the priest tried to slash his throat. They struggled for mastery on the ground, and it might have gone ill for Tuck if Will hadn't leaped on the soldier's back and stabbed him in the side of the neck.

Robyn ran to the fire and kicked over the pot. It was half-full of some unappetising brownish stew, but the turgid slop proved effective at smothering the flames.

So far, all had gone well. The sentries had been despatched without too much noise, and the outlaws were unscathed. Almost. Robyn lifted his jerkin and peered down at a ragged but shallow cut, little more than a graze, across his hip-bone. The soldier had managed to draw his knife before he died. With a little more luck he might have dragged Robyn into the afterlife with him.

Now it was down to Littiljohn to act on the signal and lead the rest of the outlaws out of the forest. While they waited, Robyn studied the village spread out below.

The rectory was some fifty paces north of the church. He guessed that the Franciscan was imposing on Richard le Wys's hospitality at the rectory, and that the Hospitallers would be there too. The barns stood dark and silent, so the remaining soldiers must be either billeted at the church or scattered about the village.

He had no time to dwell on possibilities. Littiljohn's gigantic form loomed out of the darkness, with the rest of the outlaws close behind.

"Christ," he exclaimed, glancing around at the trio of corpses, "you made quick work of this lot."

"John, take sixteen men and go down to the church," Robyn ordered, "make as much noise as you can. Smash the windows, rouse the villagers, kill every soldier you see. No mercy, save for the Franciscan. If he is there, take him prisoner. I'll take the rest and attack the rectory."

Robyn chose sixteen men and Matilda. Speed was of the essence. At some point someone in the village would notice that the beacon fire had been extinguished. The outlaws had seized the initiative. They had to cling onto it.

"Charge!" shouted Robyn, and led his men at a sprint down the hill. They shouted as they ran: "We are Robyn Hode's men, war, war, war!"

They raced into the village. Lights started to appear in the windows of the cottages and longhouses that lined the street. The rectory, a squat stone building with a tiled roof, loomed ahead.

The heavy, black-timbered door inside the porch swung open. A tall man stepped out. He wore the silvery mail and black cloak of a Hospitaller, and wore a broadsword strapped to his hip.

"On them!" Robyn shouted, quelling the fear that darted through him at the sight of the Hospitaller, "on them! Show no mercy!"

He hoped that the noise would unnerve the Franciscan and his followers, and fool them into thinking that a horde of outlaws had descended on Applewick.

The knight took one look at the hooded figures streaming towards him, calmly pushed the door shut and drew his sword. Naked steel gleamed in the moonlight. He stepped forward and took up a fighting stance, legs planted wide apart, slightly bent at the waist, sword gripped in both hands.

Robyn could not afford to falter. He also carried a sword – one of the few outlaws who did – and lugged it out as he dashed headlong at the knight.

Matilda had kept pace with him. She was armed with a knife and a hatchet, and swung the hatchet at the knight's head even as her husband stabbed clumsily at his breast.

The Hospitaller had put off his helm, and was obliged to deflect the axe before swatting away Robyn's attempt to skewer his heart. He parried both with the grace of a dancer, and responded by cutting at Matilda's legs.

She twisted away, the blade missing her by inches. Roaring in fury, Robyn aimed another stroke, this time an overhead blow at the Hospitaller's neck. Again it was turned easily. Robyn was still a clumsy swordsman, and no match for a knight trained to arms from childhood.

All around them the noise of battle raged. More voices had joined the shouts of the outlaws, mingled with war-cries and the clang and scrape of steel. It seemed the villagers had joined the fight.

Robyn had no time to feel relieved. The Hospitaller went on the attack, cutting and hacking at his opponents in a bewildering flurry of blows. Had he fought him alone, Robyn would have been swiftly cut to pieces. As it was, he gave ground, desperately parrying the blade that seemed to come at him from every angle.

A stone whistled through the air between Robyn and Matilda and cracked against the knight's skull. His eyes crossed, and he sagged onto one knee, blood pouring from the cut opened on his forehead.

Robyn hesitated. Even dazed, the knight was still dangerous. Matilda knew no such caution. Ignoring her husband's cry, she sprang in for the kill, hatchet whirling. The blade split his crown and he toppled onto his face, blood leaking from the gash. Dropping her hatchet, Matilda grasped his hair, yanked his head back and drew her knife across his throat.

Despite the noise and urgency of the battle, Robyn stared at her in disbelief. He had never suspected his wife could kill so easily. Matilda's face was twisted in a feral snarl, her hands red with the dying Hospitaller's blood.

He looked away, and saw a furious melee had erupted in the street behind him. Soldiers in white tunics and cloaks struggled hand-to-hand with outlaws and villagers. Most of the latter were young men, but there were a few women too, wielding knives and stools and other makeshift weapons, or simply tearing at the soldiers with teeth and nails. Robyn spotted a young boy curling up a sling, and nodded gratefully to him.

He detected a kind of madness in the eyes of the villagers, the same madness that had infected his wife. Something terrible had been unleashed. He decided that was the Franciscan's doing. Tuck was right. The burning of an innocent man had proved a terrible mistake, and succeeded only in lighting a flame inside the usually pliant and docile people of Applewick. The arrival of the outlaws had given them the courage to act.

The soldiers were badly outnumbered, but still fought with cool courage and professionalism, back-to-back in groups of three. Four of them had the presence of mind to fetch their horses, and came galloping down the street in an attempt to clear a path through to the rectory.

Men scattered before them, all save Littiljohn. The giant stood like a statue, huge and immovable, holding a massive oaken stave weighted at both ends with strips of iron.

The horsemen faltered at the sight of him, just as he unleashed a piercing roar and charged straight at them, stave whirling about his shaggy head. He smashed one man clean out of the saddle, causing his horse to shriek and rear onto her haunches. Another cut at Littiljohn's head. He parried the blow, grasped the soldier's cloak and dragged him down into the mud.

Emboldened by Littiljohn's courage, the outlaws and villagers swarmed back into the fight, howling like mad dogs.

The two remaining horsemen were engulfed, though their comrades bravely rushed to help, swords flickering among the surging press of bodies.

Robyn expected more Hospitallers to come spilling out of the rectory to avenge their comrade, but the door remained closed. He could not believe the warrior-monks had lost their nerve to fight, especially against such a rabble, and supposed that the Franciscan must have ordered them to stay inside to protect him.

Robyn wanted to capture the priest alive and wring some answers out of him. After that, he would hang the man from the same tree he had hanged the dead Cistercian.

Tuck came limping out of an alley, blood streaming down a sword-cut on his calf. "Robyn!" he shouted, his face ghastly pale and filmed with sweat, "there is a postern gate behind the rectory. The Franciscan escapes us."

"Attend to him," said Robyn, gripping his wife's arm and pushing her towards Tuck, "bind up that wound on his leg. Will, John – with me!"

Will and Littiljohn fought their way out of the throng and hared after Robyn as he ran down the alley. It was narrow and dark, and strewn with rubbish, but partially lit by the light streaming from the high, arched windows of the rectory to his right.

There was a high wall dividing the alley from the rectory grounds. He could hear urgent voices beyond the wall, men shouting at each other in Italian and French, and the neighing of horses.

The alley opened onto the fields north of Applewick. A heavy mist covered the ground, hiding the great mass of forest that surrounded the village. Robyn pressed his back against the wall and glanced around the corner.

As Tuck said, there was a postern gate here. As he watched, it flew open and a Hospitaller emerged, leading his horse.

"Let's have him," hissed Littiljohn, starting forward, but Robyn placed a hand flat against his chest and pushed him back.

More of the knights followed, seven in all, far too many for the outlaws to tackle. The Franciscan came last.

This was the first time Robyn had clapped eyes on the man.

Instead of the towering devil of his imagination he saw a plump, dapper little monk, his cherubic face smooth and unlined as a baby's. He had a placid and unruffled air, and betrayed no hint of panic.

His knights were mounted now. One of them barked urgently at him in French as he climbed aboard his roan mare. It seemed they wanted to make a fight of it, but the Franciscan shook his round head and muttered something negative in reply.

"He will get away!" exclaimed Littiljohn, but still Robyn refused to move. There was no help for it. The Hospitallers would slaughter them if they tried anything.

Another time, he thought regretfully as the Franciscan gave his reins a shake and spurred away into the mist, followed by his knights.

11.

Nottingham

Eustace was obliged to remain at Nottingham, held a virtual prisoner by the troops Odo de Sablé left stationed in the city after his departure to Applewick.

The initial meeting between de Sablé and the two Sheriffs had not gone well. Irritated by the inquisitor's superior and complacent attitude – he would have preferred a fire-and-brimstone preacher to deal with – Eustace had been even ruder to the man than he intended, and flatly refused to comply with any of his requests.

"You will not aid holy church?" de Sablé said in his mild voice, raising an eyebrow in surprise.

"I will aid the church in most matters," Eustace retorted, "but not some senseless witch-hunt. The Hooded Man is an outlaw, not a heretic, and should be dealt with by the secular power."

He glanced at Fitz Nicholas, who stood grey-faced and irresolute. If not for his presence, Eustace suspected, his colleague would have easily crumpled before the inquisitor.

De Sablé gave a little cough, one of his quirks that made Eustace's fists twitch. "Thus far, the secular power has been found wanting," he said, "and proved utterly incapable of preventing the attacks on church property and servants. I would not be here, otherwise."

"We are undermanned," muttered Fitz Nicholas, staring at the floor, "starved of money and men. And The Hooded Man does not lack for allies."

De Sablé spread his plump white hands. "You see, my lord Sheriff?" he said, looking at Eustace, "the evil in your lands is spreading like a cancer. How could this outlaw, this Hooded Man, possibly gain the support of knights and noblemen, unless invested with the power of the Dark One to entice them?"

"You think he is possessed by the Devil," said Eustace, not bothering to hide the sarcasm in his voice, "and this lends him powers of persuasion. Really, Father, this will not do. The plain truth of the matter is that The Hooded Man has been clever enough to raid lands granted to absentee clergymen. He gives the stolen grain away free to the poor. Thus he succeeds in attracting the nobility, aggrieved at their loss of land and revenue, and the common people. They starve, and are desperate for heroes."

De Sablé held his gaze. The inquisitor's eyes were windows into an empty soul, grey and emotionless. "You are a cynic, my lord," he said quietly, "my old master had a short way with such people. Cynicism is one of the Devil's more subtle tools. He uses it to undermine faith, and sap the strength of those who should join the army of Christ in its unending war against sin."

Eustace took that for a threat, but retained enough self-control not to rise to it. Nottingham was flooded with de Sablé's troops. He had no wish to taste the hospitality of the dungeons.

"I am no cynic, Father," he said, mustering a show of humility, "but many years of service in the shrievalty has taught me to look for the root causes of crime."

"Then you need look no further," de Sablé said blandly, "the cause is perfectly apparent to even the dullest of men. Evil lives among us. It is my task to rip it out."

The inquisitor spoke without a hint of passion, but that was merely his way. Eustace judged him the most dangerous of fanatics. Under that calm, self-possessed exterior, de Sablé was entirely consumed by God. There was no reasoning with him, and no limits to what he might do.

To argue with such a man was dangerous, and to resist him fatal. Eustace had to relent or risk destruction.

"May God aid your cause," he replied, "but, as Ralph said, there is little we can do. Our resources are stretched to breaking, merely to keep a semblance of order."

De Sablé wasn't satisfied with that, and left the greater part of his force in Nottingham as a reminder to the Sheriffs of his power and authority. Eustace was condemned to languish inside the castle, full of impotent fury at being caged while the inquisitor ran amok.

"Does it not make you angry?" he shouted at Fitz Nicholas, "by giving in to the Pope and his disgusting servant, the King has neutered us. He should have made de Sablé eat his papal bull, seal and all, and sent troops to help us deal with The Hooded Man."

"He did so before," Fitz Nicholas reminded him, "but the outlaw made fools of us all. I think His Majesty wants revenge. Mere hanging is not enough. He wants The Hooded Man to burn."

Eustace turned away in disgust. God knew he wished Robyn Hode dead, but a quick and clean death on the gallows, not this filthy method of burning alive. To him, executions were a sad necessity. Madmen like de Sablé regarded them as a glorious form of torture.

He turned his ire on the burly, hook-nosed soldier leaning nonchalantly beside the door of the Great Hall. "What in hell are you grinning at, sell-sword?" he snarled.

Fawkes de Lyons, a French soldier of fortune and captain of the King's mercenaries, had been left in command at Nottingham. Eustace regarded the man as an unofficial gaoler, and loathed the sight of him.

"A cold country, England," remarked Fawkes, glancing out of a window at the grey skies beyond, "but de Sablé will soon warm it up. I was in Hesse when Von Marburg arrived to suppress the heresies there."

He gave a low whistle. "Savage work, my lords. Some heretics were burned, others impaled, hacked apart with hot knives, or given to the mob. Von Marburg is quite the expert at rabble-rousing. I saw one recalcitrant friar, with verses from the Bible burned into his skin, torn limb from limb by a crowd of peasants while the priests looked on."

"It gives you pleasure to recall such things," Eustace said grimly. Fitz Nicholas moaned and buried his face in his hands.

Something of the mercenary's natural insouciance vanished, and his hawkish face darkened. "Merely a warning, my lord," he replied, "be thankful that de Sablé was so lenient with you. The wrath of God does not respect rank or degree. If you value your skin, do not provoke the inquisitor again."

Eustace ignored the warning. He was a man of noble family, trained to arms before ever he was appointed to the shrievalty.

To be repeatedly insulted and threatened was more than his military instincts could bear.

He sat at high table with Fitz Nicholas at supper, a tense and cheerless affair. The soldiers of the castle garrison sat apart from de Sablé's men, and both sides exchanged hostile glares. Conversation was smothered by the air of brooding violence and resentment. There was little talk even at high table, with Fitz Nicholas and his wife sunk in misery.

Eustace, for his part, was deep in thought. As one who had enforced the law all his adult life, he now contemplated breaking it. Shame and excitement warred in him, but no fear. He owed any success in his life to stubbornness rather than ability, and he stubbornly refused to be frightened of Odo de Sablé and his followers.

Fitz Nicholas was fond of music, and usually summoned his musicians to play in the hall for an hour or two after supper. There was no music tonight. After the meal was over, he made his excuses and returned with his wife to their chambers in the keep, leaving the soldiers to disperse to barracks.

Eustace's guest quarters adjoined the Great Hall, which was part of the Middle Bailey. He spent the remainder of the evening alone in his bedchamber, brooding beside the fire.

He had no intention of going to bed, and dozed in his chair until the bells of Saint Mary's sounded the midnight hour. Then he rose, splashed his face with some water from the bowl beside his bed, and donned a dark blue cloak. It was made of thick wool, and had a hood. His sword leaned against the wall in its leather sheath. He buckled it on and checked the money in the purse hanging from his belt. Ten silver shillings. More than enough to buy or hire a decent horse.

Feeling like ten kinds of fool, Eustace soft-footed to the door, carefully lifted the bar and pulled it inward. His esquire lay outside on a pallet, sound asleep. A drawn sword lay at the boy's side.

Eustace smiled. In theory the boy was guarding his master's chamber. Excess of wine had made him a poor guard tonight, unless any would-be assassins fell over him.

It suited Eustace's purpose for the boy to sleep. He carefully stepped over the slumbering body and crept down the passage.

The side-door opened out onto the Middle Bailey. Eustace hurried across this space and approached the sentry guarding the gate to the Inner.

Autumn was coming on fast. The sentry was cloaked and muffled against the cold night air.

"I need to speak to your master," Eustace said in his curtest manner, "let me through."

"The hour's late, lord," replied the guard, stifling a yawn, "can it not wait until morning? The Sheriff will be asleep."

"No, it can't." Eustace moved forward, and relief washed through him as the sentry stepped aside. Just for once, he appreciated the value of employing men who obeyed without making use of their brains.

The Inner Bailey was deserted, just as he hoped. Trembling with excitement, he strode quickly to a low doorway in the wall adjoining the keep. Inside a narrow corridor led to the ground chamber of one of the towers.

Robyn Hode's escape from the castle had been an acute embarrassment to the Sheriff of Nottingham. The outlaw's means of escape was obvious. Incredibly, no-one had previously thought to block up the doorway leading to the tunnel bored into the rock below.

"It didn't seem necessary," Fitz Nicholas said when Eustace pressed him on the matter, "nobody has escaped from the dungeons before."

It was blocked up now. The door had been ripped out and the entrance filled in with masonry. Fitz Nicholas had neglected to have it done until Eustace reminded him, just four days ago.

That was before Eustace had formulated his desperate plan. Fortunately, none of de Sablé's men were aware of the existence of the tunnel.

He ran his hands over the masonry, and grinned in the darkness as he felt the mortar was still damp.

Eustace had never done any physical work in his life. It was beneath the dignity of a nobleman, and he was amazed how quickly his hands became raw and bruised as he worked to pull away the loosest stones. He counted himself a fit man, strong and active, but soon found himself sweating and breathing hard. He drew his sword and used it to hack at the mortar.

His heart beat rapidly, and not just with the exercise and unaccustomed labour. At any moment he expected to be discovered. That would lead to some awkward explanations in the morning. Fitz Nicholas might not be the brightest of men, but even he was unlikely to swallow Eustace's claim that he had been checking the castle defences.

De Sablé might have disagreed, but God was merciful. Eustace was undisturbed as dug out a hole big enough to squeeze through. The tunnel opened before him. Eustace would have to grope through that black and sightless pit, praying that he didn't slip or lose his way.

He took a moment to compose himself, and then plunged into darkness.

12.

Odo and his remaining Hospitallers reached Nottingham after a nightmarish ride through the night. The inquisitor remained calm throughout, even though they several times lost their way in Sherwood and found themselves wandering through the seemingly endless sylvan labyrinth.

He was immune to fear, otherwise he might have prayed fervently for God to preserve him. There was no need to pray. Odo had realised long ago, as a young novice in Germany, his purpose in life. God had placed him in the world to act as a scourge of evil, and would not allow a valued servant to come to such a bitter and pointless end.

"I have survived worse than this," he informed his knights, "the heretics in Germany often laid snares, thinking to catch me unawares and put my body to the flames in mockery of holy justice. Three times the Lord delivered me from the clutches of the   mob."

"Not," he added piously, "that I had any fear of death, if God willed it so."

His words were intended to comfort the Hospitallers, but if anything had the opposite effect. The warrior-monks lacked Odo's fatalism, and cast frightened glances at the trees as they blundered through the forest, leading their horses on foot and hacking at the undergrowth with their swords.

"What ails you, men?" Odo asked as he brought up the rear, "do you fear that heretics might pursue us, or the evil spirits that lurk in the shadows? Have courage. Your blades will despatch the former, your faith the latter."

There was no pursuit. The Hooded Man and his misguided followers seemed content with their little victory at Applewick.

Odo had to admit that the ambush had taken him by surprise. The Sheriff of Yorkshire had led him to believe that the heretics in Sherwood were few in number, and could not possibly risk a fight in the open against trained soldiers.

His mind dwelled on Eustace of Lowdham. He found the man's attitude disappointing. These local officials tended to be small men, of course, lacking in mind and spirit, but he had rarely encountered such defiance before. The quaking, submissive likes of Eustace's colleague, the Sheriff of Nottingham, were the norm.

He wondered if Lowdham had deliberately misled him, in the hope that the heretics might murder Odo at Applewick. It seemed likely. That in turn gave rise to the startling possibility that the Sheriff might be in league with The Hooded Man.

What a tangled web I have wandered into, he thought, *Master Lowdham has some hard questions to answer.*

The inquisitor would get the answers he wanted, even if they had to be extracted from the subject with a degree of force. He always did. His former master had often congratulated him on his skill at interrogation.

It was almost dawn before they finally emerged from the forest, and the sun was climbing steadily into the sky by the time Nottingham's flinty walls came in sight.

Odo had not eaten since the previous afternoon. His ample guts rumbled as he and his diminished following were admitted through the city gates by the yawning sentries. He noted the sullen, resentful looks on their pinched faces. The people of Nottingham feared and distrusted the inquisitor, and wanted him gone. Odo accepted that. True servants of God could not expect to be popular.

Fawkes de Lyons met him in the Outer Bailey of the castle. The mercenary had advised Odo to take more men to Applewick, and appeared pleased that he had come to grief.

"Lost a few men, did you, Father?" he asked in a gratingly sarcastic tone. Like all sell-swords he was devoid of humility and ripe for correction. For the moment, however, Odo had need of him.

"We were ambushed," Odo replied, "I underestimated the Devil's strength. A mistake I shall not make again."

"Nor will your men. You left the city with twenty-four riders at your back, and return with just seven. It seems the Devil scored quite a victory."

A few hours alone in a room with this man, Odo decided, would soon cure him of his impudence. Along with his ability to walk and procreate.

"A temporary one," he said, brushing Fawkes aside, "like all the Dark One's victories. Now I have business with the Sheriff."

"Which one?" the mercenary called after him, "his lordship the High Sheriff of Nottinghamshire is still present, but his comrade of Yorkshire has flown the coop."

Odo halted his mare. "That cannot be. I left the greater part of my men, with you in charge, to ensure they remained in the castle."

"I am sorry to report that Lowdham slipped away at night. Perhaps the Devil spirited him away."

The inquisitor twisted in the saddle and treated Fawkes to the calm, searching look that had reduced scores of heretics to tears before they were committed to the fire.

"It amuses you to fail holy church," he said, "and to fail God. Failure, as you should well know, does not go unpunished. I believe you served for a time in Germany."

Odo could hardly have made the threat more explicit. It had the desired effect. Fawkes dropped his gaze, and some of the bounce went out of him.

"My apologies, Father," he said sullenly, "I spoke out of turn. It is true that Eustace of Lowdham escaped from the castle last night. I did not know he had gone until cock-crow, and sent riders to search for him. They have not come back yet."

"Pray that they find him, de Lyons," said Odo, turning away, "pray that they find him."

Satisfied that he had broken one man, he made his way to the keep to work on another. He regarded the Sheriff of Nottingham as a sluggish, lack-witted incompetent, and was surprised to find the man awake and waiting for him in the Great Hall. The hall was otherwise empty, save for a few dogs snuffling about among the rushes, and a kitchen-boy working to light the fire in the massive hearth.

"You are up at an early hour, my lord Sheriff," said Odo as he bustled into the hall, followed by the Hospitallers, "a shame you were not quite so alert last night. I hear your colleague decided to leave us."

Fitz Nicholas was slumped at one of the long benches below

high table. There was clearly no need to break him. Recent events had done the work already. He was a limited man, only fitted to catching petty thieves and cut-purses. Hooded men and papal inquisitors were quite beyond him.

"I knew nothing of Lowdham's intentions," he mumbled. "As Christ is my Saviour, I swear I did not know. I would have restrained him."

Something about Fitz Nicholas reminded Odo of a frightened hog going to slaughter. Confident of his mastery, the inquisitor stepped up to high table and planted himself in the Sheriff's chair.

"Tell me how Lowdham got out," he said, folding his hands across his belly, "I assume he did not simply vanish into thin air."

Fitz Nicholas grimaced and rubbed his forehead before answering. "The tunnel, Father," he said wretchedly, "the same tunnel that Robert Hode escaped from, just a few weeks back. I had ordered it blocked up, but the mortar had not set. Eustace worked the stones loose."

"I see. Yet, despite knowing that the wall was not secure, you failed to have it guarded?"

Fitz Nicholas swallowed. There was a faint patina of sweat on his brow. Odo smiled to see it. He derived much quiet enjoyment from inspiring fear. His only greater pleasures in life were the ecstasy of self-flagellation and the inflicting of pain on others.

"It didn't seem necessary," the Sheriff gabbled, "we only have two prisoners in the dungeon. They have been there for months, and barely have the strength to walk."

Odo let him stew for a moment. He was aware of this Robert Hode – Robyn, as he was known to the peasants – and how the tale of his escape from Nottingham Castle had given rise to a number of local rhymes and ballads. Trivial, foolish stuff, fit only for the ears of rustics.

A new thought occurred to him. "This man Hode," he said, "what became of him after he got out of the castle?"

"No-one knows for certain, Father, but Eustace suspects him to The Hooded Man."

"And what do you think?"

"I...I think it quite likely. Hode is a Yorkshireman. Eustace knew him of old, and said he was a notorious troublemaker. He used to run with an outlaw named Hobbe of Wetherby, until the latter was caught and executed. A dangerous man, capable of anything."

Odo contemplated his nails for a moment. Then he scraped back his chair, stood up, sighed heavily, and leaned his palms on the table.

"You are an even greater fool than I took you for, Fitz Nicholas," he said, "Lowdham practically admitted his guilt to your face, and you failed to spot it. I am tempted to write to King Henry and recommend that you be stripped of office."

Fitz Nicholas gaped at him, jaw hanging open, eyes full of misery and confusion. "Forgive me, Father," he whined, "I don't understand."

Odo was not a demonstrative man. Displays of passion, Von Marburg had taught him, were a waste of vital energy. Now he found it necessary to smash his plump fist on the table and raise his voice.

"Lowdham practically admitted that he knew who the Hooded Man was," he roared, his voice making the rafters tremble, "and then he escaped using the same tunnel as Robert Hode. Can you not see, you blind idiot, that they are allies? Lowdham even told you that they knew each other in Yorkshire. What more did you need, a signed confession?"

He shut his eyes, so he didn't have to look at the Sheriff, and made a great effort to control himself. It was tempting, so very tempting, to accuse Fitz Nicholas of consorting with the heretics and put him on trial. The stench of his roasting fat would do much to restore Odo's good humour.

Not for the first time, Odo savoured the power invested in him by Pope and King. He could do more or less as he pleased, but it was important to concentrate on the right targets. Burning a man out of petty spite would get him no closer to ridding England of evil.

At least he now knew for certain where heresy lay. "Did Eustace escape alone?" he demanded.

"Yes, Father," Fitz Nicholas replied, "he left his squire and his escort behind. They claim he did not confide in them."

"Have them arrested and detained in your dungeon. Put a double guard on it this time. We want no further break-outs. I will question them all upon my return."

"Return…return from where?"

Odo drew himself up to his full, not very impressive height. "Fawkes de Lyons has men out searching for Lowdham," he said, "but I doubt they will root him out. He will be in Sherwood, conspiring with his heretic friends. Once he thinks it is safe, Lowdham will make his way back to York. He still has authority there."

His voice rose to a shout. "I see now why the Holy Father sent me here. The north of England is foul with heresy and corruption. Those who are tasked with keeping the law of God and man either fail in their duty, or join forces with evildoers. The tumour must be cut out before it can spread. I mean to ride out in force, no half-measures this time, and purify every town and village between here and York with fire."

"The Hooded Man and his accomplices will come out to face me, in the open, or every one of their friends will go to the stake. Any who sing rhymes of Robyn Hode shall suffer the same fate. I shall follow the example of the great Conqueror, and leave not a stick or stone standing, nor man nor beast alive, until the Devil is driven out!"

13.

The outlaws lost four men in the fight at Applewick. Twice that number suffered injuries ranging from minor to serious. Robyn felt the loss of the four keenly, but the villagers had fared worse. Nine of their young men had fallen to the swords of de Sablé's soldiers.

"The village will struggle to survive without them," he said to Matilda, "unless I plead with their lord to transfer some men from his other manors."

He found it distasteful to talk of men in such terms, as though they were mere cattle to be moved from place to place as their lord willed, but that was the reality. In small country villages like Applewick, where all the labour was done by hand, the presence of enough strong, healthy young men was vital.

The lord of Applewick was Sir Robert Deyville, who Robyn had some influence with. Since their first meeting at the cross near Blidworth, Deyville had twice allowed the outlaws to shelter at his castle at Egmanton, and once further north, on his manor of Adingfleet in the marshy Isle of Axholme, at the junction of the Trent and the Humber. He was a hard man, a typically ruthless and self-interested Norman baron, but not entirely devoid of compassion.

"Deyville will not allow his serfs to starve," Matilda assured her husband, "where is the sense in that?"

"He may have to give some of them up to the gallows, after this night's work," he replied gloomily.

Victory over the inquisitor gave Robyn little joy. Too many had died, including the sixteen Italian crossbowmen. In the grey, pitiless light of morning Applewick looked like a charnel house. Bodies were still scattered about the street, though the survivors had started to clear them away. The air was full of the groans of the wounded and dying, and the weeping of the bereaved.

Tuck and Richard le Wys had turned the church into a makeshift hospital, and were working furiously to save as many lives as they could. Robyn had been surprised and gratified to discover that le Wys, whom he had regarded as a typically venal priest, was prepared to put aside his hatred of the outlaws for the sake of his parishioners.

"These people are in my charge," he had declared, rolling up his sleeves, "if I fail them now, what am I?"

These words resonated with Robyn. Whatever he did, it seemed he was destined to fail, or rather, to fail others. In his heart he knew this was unavoidable. Men died in battle. Those who gave their lives at Applewick had done so freely, striking a blow for a cause they believed was just.

"If only we had captured the Franciscan," he said, "that would have been something. We could have held him for ransom and as surety for the lives of the villagers. Now he will go back to Nottingham and summon the Sheriff to help him avenge his defeat."

"Then we will take the villagers into Sherwood," said Matilda, "and shelter them there until the storm has passed."

Robyn didn't relish the thought of having so many extra mouths to feed and house, but there seemed no alternative. His conscience would not allow him to abandon the people of Applewick to their fate.

The outlaws stayed for another two days, helping the inhabitants to bury and mourn their dead. Robyn despatched men into the forest to watch for any sign of approaching troops. None came, and he briefly allowed himself the luxury of thinking that the Franciscan had lost his nerve and fled Nottinghamshire.

On the morning of the third day, while he was at breakfast in the rectory, one of his scouts returned unexpectedly.

"What is it, Much?" Robyn demanded, looking up from his gruel with concern at the wild-eyed, shivering youth standing in the doorway. Much was one of the recent recruits and the unfortunate owner of a stupid face. In fact he was a good deal brighter than he looked, big and powerfully-built, and the second strongest man in the band after Littiljohn.

He was also not easily scared, but now he visibly trembled, his ape-like features white as fresh milk. "Fire and smoke," he gasped, struggling to get the words out, "fire and smoke!"

Robyn glanced at Tuck, who rose and put a kind arm around Much's broad shoulders. "Come and sit down, lad," he said in the gentle voice he reserved for his patients, "have a drink and soothe your nerves. Take your time."

Richard le Wys made room for the big man on the bench, while Matilda poured him a generous measure of the vicar's limited supply of Rhenish wine. Much accepted the cup with a shaking hand and tossed the contents down his well-muscled throat.

Robyn waited patiently while the young man gulped and wiped his mouth. An uneasy silence reigned in the hall as everyone waited for him to speak.

"Fire and smoke," he whispered at last, so quietly Robyn had to lean over the table to hear, "the land is in flames. The skies are black with smoke. The stench...you can't breathe for the stench of burning!"

"Where did you see the fires?" asked Tuck, still in the same gentle tone. Much screwed his eyes shut before replying.

"I rode south," he went on, "a couple of miles from here. I would have stopped, but saw smoke on the horizon, just a faint wisp or two, rising above the trees near Newstead. I ventured as close to the village as I dared."

His eyes snapped open. "The smoke was thickest there," he said dreamily, "great black clouds of the stuff. I could smell it over a mile off. The village was burning. I heard screams."

Newstead was just a few miles north of Nottingham. "How close did you get?" asked Robyn, trying to keep his voice calm and low, "what else did you see? Was the Franciscan there?"

"I didn't see him, but those horse-soldiers with the black cloaks were there. There were others as well, so many soldiers, like devils among the flames. People were trying to get out, to escape the fires, but the soldiers didn't let them. They barred the gates and slew anyone who tried to climb over the stockade."

"Little children," he said, gaping witlessly at Robyn, "the black-cloaks were killing children."

Matilda passed him the wine-jug. He grabbed it and slugged down the contents while the others stared at each other.

"The Italian has struck back quickly," murmured le Wys,

"who in God's name is he, and why does he hate us so?"

"A papal servant of some kind, of that I have no doubt," said Tuck, "one of Pope Gregory's new inquisitors, perhaps. We have all heard the stories of the horrors they commit in France and Germany. I can scarcely believe that King Henry would allow them into England."

"The king is a slave to the papacy," Robyn said scornfully, "the Pope merely has to whistle, and Henry comes to heel, like a good dog."

He pushed back his bench and stood up. "This is my doing," he said, "if I had not started this foolish war against the church, the people of Applewick and Newstead would not be suffering. Now I must put an end to what I started."

"You will not give yourself up to him," Matilda said flatly, "I will not allow you."

"I don't mean to. Judging from what Much saw, it is too late for that. The Devil is loose in England, disguised as God's servant."

Robyn moved swiftly. Leaving Littiljohn in command, with orders to take the villagers into Sherwood, he rode out of Applewick with just a few men at his back and headed for Newstead. His intention was to see the destruction for himself.

They had not ridden two miles before faint wisps of smoke became visible to the south, drifting above the canopy of the forest.

"There is Newstead," said Much, pointing at each wisp in turn, "and there is Papplewick, and there Ravenshead. They all burn."

Robyn had feared the worst, and it had come to pass. The inquisitor was steadily moving north from Nottingham, burning and destroying every settlement in his path.

"He has run mad," said Will.

"No," Robyn replied, "that is too easy. There must be some reason behind it. Perhaps the Franciscan means to draw us out of Sherwood again. Much said he has come in force this time."

"Many soldiers," said Much, who had not yet recovered from his shock, "more than I could count."

"More than nine, then," said Robyn with a smile. The joke

creaked, but it was something, and better than dwelling on the evil that confronted them.

Robyn often felt the burden of leadership, pressing down like a physical weight on his shoulders, but never more so than now. Six frightened faces looked at him, trusting him to come up with a plan.

He had already thought of one. "Come," he said, turning his horse, "we can do no good here."

The outlaws turned north, following the road that led to Sir Robert Deyville's castle at Egmanton.

Deyville was a minor baron, unable to afford rebuilding his scattered castles in stone. Thus Egmanton Castle was much the same as it had been in his grandfather's day, an old-fashioned motte and bailey fortress built entirely in timber. It overlooked the village, a peaceful little place enclosed by a wooden stockade, though the puffs of smoke rising from the cottages put Robyn in mind of the fires raging to the south.

He rode to the village gates and hailed the men on the earth and timber parapet, asking to speak to their lord.

"Who might you be?" asked one, running a suspicious eye over the outlaws, "Sir Robert is a private man, and must not be disturbed without good reason."

"Your lord knows me. Tell him that Robyn Hode is at his gates."

The sentry looked dubious, but stumped away to fetch his lord. Robyn and his men were not kept waiting long before the gates swung inwards, and Deyville cantered out on a big chestnut destrier.

The hard-faced knight was as taciturn as ever. "Expected you," he snapped, "heard about the skirmish at Applewick. Seen and smelled the fires. Madness. Follow me."

He spoke as one used to command, and didn't even check to see if the outlaws obeyed as he wheeled his horse and rode back into the village. Robyn exchanged wry glances with Will and led his men after him.

The castle stables and the hall were among the outbuildings packed together in the crowded lower bailey, set on a man-made hill above the village. Deyville's grooms saw to the horses, while he took the outlaws into the hall.

This was a long, low building, more like a massive barn than the princely grandeur of the Great Hall at Nottingham Castle. It was old, dating back to the founding of the castle, and the rafters supporting the high, arched roof were blackened with age and wood-smoke. A few battered shields bearing the Deyville arms hung from the walls, alongside dusty and moth-eaten friezes and tapestries displaying faded hunting and battle scenes.

It was also empty of furniture, save for a long, narrow table in the middle, upon which was rolled out a map of northern England. Three armed men stood by the table, marked out as knights by their twinkling mail and the arms on their surcoats.

Robyn recognised two of the knights as Sir Robert de Ros and Sir Richard de Riparia, who he had met at the Blidworth cross in Sherwood. He exchanged wary greetings with them, but did not recognise the third.

"Sir Robert de Everingham," Deyville said gruffly, "a knight of Yorkshire, and hereditary Keeper of Sherwood Forest."

Everingham was a tall, strikingly handsome man with thinning hair and a pointed tuft of beard. "Robyn Hode," he said with a thin smile, bowing slightly from the waist, "it seems the world has turned upside down. My duty is to hunt the likes of you, but for now it seems we must be allies."

Robyn coloured slightly. He had heard of Everingham, whose family were responsible for protecting the game in Sherwood. So far the Keeper's officers in the forest had let the outlaws alone. Robyn was happy for this arrangement to continue.

"My lord," he said with a polite nod, and turned to Deyville, "I did not come here to detain or embarrass you, but to ask for your help in defeating our common enemy."

Deyville held up a hand. "I understand why you are here," he replied. "The Pope has set a mad dog loose in our land. He must be put down before he destroys any more villages and crops."

Robyn sent up a silent prayer in thanks to the Virgin. He had wondered how Deyville might receive him, and if he would have to beg for help. The Norman barons that ruled England were scarcely more trustworthy than their kinsmen in the church. Robyn's darkest fear was that Deyville might simply arrest the outlaws and hand them over to the Franciscan.

"I summoned these men here," Deyville added, indicating his companions, "for a council of war. I have also sent messengers to several other knights and barons in Nottinghamshire and Yorkshire, friends and kinsmen of mine."

"What about the Sheriffs?"

"Useless. Fitz Nicholas hides in his castle, and Lowdham has disappeared. They say that he argued with de Sablé, and was locked up in a dungeon for his pains."

Robyn had not known the Franciscan's name until now. It meant nothing to him, but Tuck gasped and made the sign of the cross against evil.

"Odo de Sablé," he exclaimed, "so that is who we have to deal with. Rome could not have sent a worse man, save Von Marburg himself."

"You know of him, then?" asked Everingham, clearly surprised that this underfed hedge-priest might have knowledge of the wider world.

"Indeed, my lord. Tales of his zeal and cruelty even reached the cloisters at Fountains Abbey when I was a novice there. Sir Robert described him as a mad dog. I cannot think of a better description."

"It is well to know one's enemy," said Deyville. He turned to the map and stabbed his index finger at certain points north of Nottingham. "My scouts informed me that de Sablé marched out of Nottingham yesterday morning, at the head of two hundred and fifteen knights, sergeants and crossbowmen. He has left a trail of fire and slaughter on his march north, and lingered over the destruction of three villages."

"My villages," said Everingham, his handsome face flushing with anger, "de Sablé's wolves descended on them before I knew what was happening. I rode out to defend Newstead, but my handful of squires and archers could do nothing against so many. We turned back."

"Tell me," asked Deyville, glancing sidelong at Robyn, "what happened at Applewick? Does the place still stand?"

"It does," Robyn replied awkwardly, "though there were a few casualties. I am sorry for that, but de Sablé had already murdered one of your serfs and would have killed again if we had not driven him out."

"Never mind your blasted serfs, Robert," Sir Richard de Riparia said hotly, "we will all suffer if this whoreson priest is not stopped. King Henry must learn that the north will not endure this kind of treatment."

The knights murmured in agreement. "Henry has a short memory," remarked Everingham, "our fathers almost toppled his from the throne. It is time to demonstrate that our swords have not rusted in their scabbards."

"Down to business, then," said Deyville, "I propose we evacuate every settlement between here and the Yorkshire border. Take the young men who can fight. The rest can scatter into the forests, or go wherever they think best until the fighting is done."

"That means abandoning your lands and villages," said Robyn, surprised that the barons were prepared to retreat before the enemy so easily.

"I know," said Deyville with a shrug, "but we haven't got enough men to stand against de Sablé. Between us we can raise a hundred sergeants and archers, not counting the serfs we can arm. How many have you got?"

So that was it. The barons needed Robyn's outlaws as reinforcements. "Less than thirty who are fit to fight," he replied, "the skirmish at Applewick was a bloody one. Most are peasant boys. We have few horses and no armour."

Deyville's face creased in disappointment. "Not enough. Nowhere near enough. De Sablé outnumbers us over two to one, and his men are all soldiers, with good gear and horses."

"We retreat north," said Ros, drawing his dagger and tracing a line along the map from the northern part of Sherwood to the edge of Yorkshire, "our messengers should have reached the Percies and Fitzwalter by now. They will join us. We can meet them as they march south, and then turn to face the enemy."

Deyville stared at the map. "Agreed," he murmured, "they should be able to raise enough men to balance the odds. And we can choose our ground. If de Sablé continues to march north, we can ambush him on the way."

"Your men," he said, nodding at Robyn, "can harry them as they come up the Great North Road. Thin them out with a few arrows, and then vanish into the forests."

"My gamekeepers tell me you are quite expert at such tactics," Everingham said sourly.

Robyn hesitated. He had hoped to enlist the aid of Deyville and the other northern barons, since only they possessed the military strength to resist de Sablé, but now found himself being given orders. They naturally assumed that he, a mere commoner, would comply.

This is a war I started, he thought, *and until it is won, I must set aside my pride.*

"Very well," he said, "we will do our best to hurt de Sablé before battle is joined."

14.

Matilda chose to stay behind at Applewick, helping Richard le Wys to tend those casualties too badly hurt to be moved. She also helped to take down the charred remnants of John Maker from the stake, and to dig a pit in the village cemetery for his burial.

She refused to look at le Wys as he muttered the last rites over the freshly-dug grave. They, and two of the village youths who had also volunteered to stay behind, were the only mourners.

"This Franciscan must be a very persuasive man," she said to the vicar later, after they had done what they could for the wounded and dying in the church.

He was washing his bloody hands in a bowl of water heated over the fire, and looked up sharply at her. "You blame me for John's death," he said, "you think I should have opposed Odo de Sablé's judgment, and refused to let him burn an innocent man?"

"That is exactly what I think."

Le Wys paused to dry his hands. "You are young," he murmured, gazing at the streaks of blood on the cloth, "you know nothing of the nature of power, and what it can do. One does not resist a man like de Sablé. He enjoys the favour of the Pope. As a man of God, my duty was to obey him."

"And what of your duty to your parishioners?"

He looked up and fastened his gaze on a crucifix hanging from a nail on the wall. It bore a tiny pewter Christ writhing in his death-throes, his naked hands and feet impaled on the cross.

"For all I know, John Maker was in need of purifying," he said in a hollow voice, "the purpose of burning the flesh is to cleanse the soul and save the heretic from damnation. That is my consolation."

"May it comfort you at night," she spat. For the rest of the evening Matilda avoided him, and spent the night in one of the abandoned cottages. There she spent a largely sleepless night on a dirty and uncomfortable mattress, much disturbed by dreams of Robyn tied to a stake and calling her name in vain as the flames rose round him.

She was woken at dawn by Will, who in his usual charmless manner nudged her awake with the toe of his boot.

"Up, slug-a-bed," he said, "we have work to do, and men to kill."

Matilda sat up, yawning and knuckling her tired eyes. "Will," she said blearily, "what is happening? Where is Robyn? Is he safe?"

"Safe enough when I left him. He and the others returned to camp last night. Come, I will explain on the way."

She struggled to her feet and followed him into a cold, ghostly dawn. The village was silent as the grave, the thatched roofs and rough wattle-and-daub walls of the houses shrouded in mist.

Will had brought two horses and tethered them in the stables beside the smithy. One was Robyn's courser. The sleek grey beast neighed and tossed her head in recognition of her master's wife.

"I still have work to do here, in Applewick," she said as Will untied the courser's reins and tossed them to her, "three men still lie sick, and one is unlikely to live another day. I swore to be at his side."

"You should not swear oaths, then," replied Will, who was not over-burdened with sentiment. His voice was terse, and his usual carefree and sardonic manner absent.

He was obviously in no mood for argument, and Matilda's desire to see Robyn overcame her duty to the sick. Comforting herself with the thought that Le Wys and his attendants would care for them, she led the courser outside and climbed nimbly into the saddle.

They rode at a fast canter through the silent, mist-clotted morning, following the side-road that led from Applewick to the highway. A strange hush pervaded the forest, as though some spell had been laid over it. Nameless fears gnawed at Matilda, and no words were exchanged until they reached the winding paths that eventually led to the outlaw camp.

"You said we had men to kill," she said as they led their horses on foot through a difficult patch of ground, "what did you mean? Does Robyn mean to fight the Franciscan?"

Will nodded. "He does. Yesterday he enlisted the help of some of the barons. Sir Robert Deyville and his ilk. Or rather, they enlisted us."

He went on to explain how the barons had evacuated their villages and retreated north to join their allies in Yorkshire. Meanwhile the outlaws were charged with the task of harrying Odo de Sablé's little army as it marched north.

"We are to do as much damage as we can," he said, "and make the Italians bleed before they reach the borders of Yorkshire. Deyville and his northerners will confront them there."

Matilda pictured the opposing lines of mailed horsemen, spears and helms gleaming in the sun, banners waving. It was a strangely magnificent image, straight out of the tales of chivalry, and made her shudder.

"It sounds like a war," she said.

"And so it is. One we must play our part in."

Nothing more was said until they reached the camp. Here was a bustle of activity. Men clustered around a great pile of weapons set out on the ground beside the Major Oak. There were spears and knives, staves and clubs, hunting bows and sheaves of arrows in plenty, along with the swords and crossbows captured from de Sablé's men at Applewick.

Robyn, Tuck and Littiljohn were sharing out the weapons among the men. "Bow and stave for you, Much," Robyn was saying to the giant youth, "you have no training with the sword, and are more likely to cut your own foot off with it than hurt an enemy."

He stopped as Matilda and Will entered the clearing. His gaunt face lit up with joy, and he gathered her up in a fierce embrace.

"Matilda," he said warmly, "my wife, my love, my own. A cold bed on hard ground was my lot last night. I could not sleep for thinking of you."

"Nor I you," she replied, smiling down at him, "I never want to suffer such dreams again. Will tells me we are going to war."

He gently set her down. "We are. Even now de Sablé and his men march north. They left Newstead a lifeless, smoke-blackened ruin. Some few of the people managed to escape into

91

Sherwood, but the rest were slaughtered like beasts. All in the name of God."

"No God that I recognise," said Tuck. Matilda noticed him wince when he bent to pick up a spear, and the fresh blood trickling down the bandage she had tied around his wounded leg.

"You should be resting," she said crossly, kneeling to inspect the bandage, "else this cut may turn bad, and then we shall have a one-legged priest to minister to us."

Tuck grumbled, but eventually consented to take the weight off his leg and sit quietly with his back to the oak, between two of the enormous spreading roots. Matilda fetched some water from the stream nearby and washed his wound.

"You are in no fit state to fight, Tuck," said Robyn, "when we move out, you will stay here and rest."

He held up one brown hand to still his friend's protests. "Not another word. Pray for us, if you like. Someone should."

Attending to Tuck helped to distract Matilda from the latest danger her husband was about to throw himself into. As ever, he was the moving spirit of the outlaws, joking with them and speaking words of encouragement as he handed out weapons.

There was a strange excitement about them, an eagerness to be off to war, like hounds straining at the leash. Matilda remembered the terrible aftermath of the skirmish at Applewick, the bleeding and crippled bodies, men begging for death as they lay in pools of gore and filth, and wondered at their folly.

"Twenty-eight," said Robyn when all his available followers were armed and assembled in the clearing, "it will have to do. God grant that the barons do not fail us."

Matilda stood up. "Twenty-nine," she said firmly, "I am coming with you."

"No. The people of the village are camped a little way off. Some of the older ones are sick. I promised you would stay to nurse them."

She had to laugh at his duplicity. "Clever," she said, "you knew I would not obey you this time, and so bind me with promises."

"As you did to me," he replied quietly. The clearing and the outlaws seemed to fade away, and there was just the two of them, together in Sherwood.

Matilda was determined not to weep. She dug her nails into her palms to force back the tears. "If you go now, I fear I shall not see you again on this earth. God wishes to break us apart."

He gently stroked her arm. "One cannot fight against God," he said, "I know that now. We were the King and Queen of summer. Summer is almost gone."

The spell broke. He stepped away from her, one tear glistening on his ruddy cheek, and turned back to his men. They all knew their orders, and followed Robyn in silence as he jogged away into the forest.

When they were gone, Matilda dealt with her sense of desolation by fetching bread and ale for Tuck, and watching while he ate.

"Go and see to the villagers," he said through a mouthful of hard rye bread, "I am not going to die if you take your eyes off me."

"Leave him in my care," said Adam of the Dale, who also sat with his back against the oak, "I will sing to him, and he can teach me a few psalms."

Adam had been left behind as a non-combatant. Nobody had ever seen him fight, and he only carried a weapon when hunting. The sight of blood, he was fond of declaring, made him forget his art. His chief role in the band was to keep them entertained and compose verses in Robyn's honour.

Matilda left them to it and went to see how the people of Applewick were faring. They were not quite as wretched as she expected. Their reeve had taken charge, and organised the youngest and fittest of the villagers into groups, ordering them to light fires, erect rough shelters with the wood and canvas supplied by the outlaws, and place the sick together in a tent.

"We don't mean to be a burden," he told Matilda, "as soon as the foreigners are defeated, we will return to our village."

Like so many, he seemed to have absolute faith in Robyn. There was no question in his mind that the outlaws would win, and that afterwards they could all return to their normal lives.

Matilda felt almost ashamed at entertaining doubts, but nothing could wipe the image from her mind of Robyn burning at the stake.

We were the King and Queen of summer. Summer is almost gone.

She moved about the sick-tent, grim and terse as she checked pulses and doled out advice. There was not much to be done. One old woman who had not left Applewick for years had suffered an attack of arthritis, and could only lie on her back and wait for the pain to pass. Two young men had still not recovered from a broken arm and fractured wrist, taken during the skirmish. Matilda checked their dressings and ordered them to sleep as much as possible.

"Gladly, madam," one of them said, with a sly wink at his companion. Matilda smiled wanly and left the tent.

"Peace and rest, that's all they need," she said to the reeve, and hurried away before he could ask questions. The stares of the villagers were wearing on her nerves. She could overhear some of the younger women gossiping about her. To them Matilda was not a person in her own right, but merely Robyn Hode's wife.

The outlaw camp lay some quarter of a mile away. Adam's powerful voice carried through the trees, butchering some Latin psalm. His singing lifted Matilda's heart a little, and she was sorry when he stopped.

All was quiet when she reached the clearing. Adam had vanished, and Tuck sat slumped against the oak, sound asleep. Matilda smiled. She felt oddly protective towards the priest, who she regarded as something of a father-figure, even though they were only a few years separated in age. Save when he was in his cups, Tuck carried himself with a gravity that made him seem much older.

Knowing she was being foolish, Matilda decided to check on his wound again. She trod softly over to the tree, not wishing to wake him, and stopped dead. Her blood turned to ice.

Tuck was not asleep, but unconscious, maybe dead. His head was broken, bright red arterial blood leaking from a savage gash on his scalp. More flowed from his ears, nose and mouth.

Matilda opened her mouth to scream for help, but a strong hand gripped her shoulder and spun her around.

She had just enough time to see Adam, his girlish face flushed, teeth gritted in a bestial snarl, and to raise her arm in a futile attempt to ward off the club he wielded in his right hand.

The club smashed against her brow, and she knew nothing more.

15.

Robyn drew the bow-string back to his chest, took careful aim, and let fly. The arrow flew straight and true, but the soldier got his shield up in time, and it deflected harmlessly off the iron rim.

He cursed and reached for another arrow from the sheaf thrust into his belt. A thick patch of briars and thorns hid him from the road, about twenty feet away, where de Sablé's men were exposed to arrows from all directions.

The outlaws had fallen on the inquisitor's rearguard along the stretch of road between Worksop and Tickhill. Thick plumes of smoke from burning villages and farmsteads bruised the sky to the south, casting a pall over the running battle in the forest. Robyn had decided to risk an ambush before the Italians reached the safety of the massive royal castle at Tickhill, where the constable would be obliged to open his gates to receive them.

De Sablé was evidently something of a soldier as well as a churchman, and had divided his men into three battles or divisions. He rode in the vanguard, his monkish habit swapped for a mail hauberk and a steel helm, surrounded by the Hospitallers and their esquires. The lighter-armed crossbowmen rode in the centre, three abreast, while the rearguard was made up of the footmen, sergeants in padded tunics armed with spears and large, triangular shields.

Six of the sergeants guarded a wagon that creaked along in the rear. It carried no baggage or supplies, but a large wooden crucifix, some ten feet high, that Robyn assumed to be de Sablé's talisman. The crucifix was painted black, and Sherwood rang to the doleful sound of plainchant as the little army trudged northwards. Every man added his voice to the hymn, their master's powerful baritone foremost among them.

Three sergeants lay dead on the road, throats and eyes transfixed by arrows. Robyn's men were strung out in the woods either side of the road, loosing off shots before vanishing into the undergrowth, as he had trained them.

He broke cover, took aim, and shot. This time his arrow struck an Italian in the leg, just below the knee. The wounded man yelled and fell onto his backside, frantically tugging at the shaft as dark blood gushed down his leg.

Despite being taken by surprise, the soldiers were brave and professional, and refused to panic. Their captain, a stocky, hook-nosed man with a drooping grey moustache, was screaming at them, trying to form a wall of shields around the wagon. The wooden cross was precious, it seemed, and had to be defended.

Robyn glanced to his right. Some of the crossbowmen had dismounted and were streaming down the road to aid their comrades. They stopped to load their cumbersome weapons, jamming their feet into the stirrups and fumbling darts into the grooves.

"Bring them down!" Robyn screamed. At the same time he notched another arrow, drew back the string and loosed, all in one smooth movement. His arrow took one of the crossbowmen in the shoulder, flinging him backwards.

A few of the outlaws heard their master's command and turned to shoot. Two more Italians fell, but the rest held their ground. They took careful aim at the men in the woods. Their captain barked the order to shoot.

Robyn dropped onto his face. He had seen what crossbows were capable of. The stubby, evil-looking darts could punch through steel and flesh with ease. He winced as a shriek of pain erupted behind him. Someone had been too slow to duck.

A shadow fell over Robyn, blotting out the sun, and Littiljohn's enormous bulk landed beside him with a thump that made the ground shake.

"It's Will," the big man said breathlessly, "dart got him in the shoulder. I told one of the lads to help him to safety."

Robyn nodded in approval. He half-rose, and peered through the twisting web of brambles and ferns. His men were flitting like shadows through the woods, keeping up a steady rain of arrows on the hapless Italians.

The sergeants had formed a tight square around the wagon, crouched well behind their shields. Caught in the open, the crossbowmen enjoyed no such protection as they worked frantically to reload.

"Ignore the shields!" Robyn howled. "Shoot the crossbows! Shoot them down!"

His voice cracked as he strove to be heard. His men in the trees opposite were either deaf or stubborn, and continued to waste their arrows on the line of upraised shields.

If the outlaws would not listen, they would have to be shown by example. Snatching up his bow, Robyn ran lightly down the shallow bank towards the edge of the woods. Littiljohn pounded along close behind him.

"Careful, Robyn," the giant panted, "not too close."

He almost ran into Robyn as the latter stopped suddenly, his head cocked to one side. The shrill blast of a trumpet sounded to their right, further up the road, once, twice, and was accompanied by the thunder of galloping hoofs.

The Hospitallers charged into view, bright swords gleaming in their mailed fists, cloaks flying about them like bat-wings. They made no attempt to warn or avoid the crossbowmen in their path, but simply rode through them. Most of the Italians scattered in time, but one was ridden down, his back broken and skull trampled to fragments.

Robyn strung an arrow and sent a hurried shot flying at the leading knight. He might as well have tossed a pebble at him. The arrow ricocheted off the knight's helm, not even slowing his progress, and spun away into the woods.

A massive hand closed on Robyn's arm. "Back," grunted Littiljohn, heaving his master up the slope. "We can't fight these bastards in the open."

Littiljohn possessed terrifying strength, and Robyn was dragged away like a small child in his father's grip. He kept his eyes fixed on the road, watching as the Hospitallers split up and plunged recklessly into the woods flanking the road.

Robyn tore his arm free and reached for the hunting horn that hung from a baldric over his shoulder. Littiljohn was right. They could not hope to beat the Hospitallers at close quarters. Better to keep a distance and shoot them down from afar.

He raised the horn to his lips and blew three deep blasts that echoed and re-echoed through the surrounding forest. Two blasts was the signal to attack, three to retreat. The outlaws had done enough damage for now, and fulfilled Deyville's request to thin the Italian ranks a little.

Robyn felt a surge of adrenaline as he turned and ran. Here, on the cusp of death, he felt alive in a way he had rarely experienced before. It was the joy of battle, the madness that overcomes men in combat.

He swarmed up a muddy bank, using stones jutting from the earth as handholds, and grabbed a hanging branch to pull himself to the top. There he turned and plucked an arrow from his belt.

One of the Hospitallers was below, trying to urge his horse up the slope. She refused to go, tossing her head and neighing in panic as her forelegs sank into the soft earth.

Robyn's hunting bow lacked the power to send an arrow through the knight's coat of mail. The only option was to shoot his horse and then stick a knife through the narrow eye-slit of his helm as he lay helpless on the ground.

Littiljohn already had the same idea, and was notching an arrow when three men exploded from the woods and converged on the knight, baying like wolves.

"Get back, you fools!" Robyn screamed. The three men were the newest members of the band, raw youths, two of them armed with long staves, the third with a sword.

Much was the third man. Robyn had ordered him to choose some other weapon, but the ugly youth's vanity had overcome his common sense.

Littiljohn's arrow plunged into the horse's rear even as her master dragged savagely on her reins, dragging the beast in a half-circle to present her flank to their attackers. She screamed in pain, but the knight kept a tight control on her, and met Much's clumsy attempt at a thrust with a blow that jarred the young man's wrists and sent the sword spinning from his hands.

Robyn drew and shot. His arrow hit the wounded horse in the neck, piercing a vein. She staggered and collapsed onto her side, shrieking horribly as her blood pumped into the red earth. Her rider, his sword raised to strike off Much's head, was thrown clear.

He rolled as he landed, and was quickly on his feet again, none the worse for the fall. Two of the youths charged at him, howling in triumph, staves ready to beat him into pulp.

The knight's sword traced a complex pattern in the air, too quick for Robyn's eye to follow. One of the youths buckled to his knees, whistling like a kettle coming to the boil, hands pressed over the neat slash in his belly. His innards squirmed out of the hole like worms, regardless of his desperate efforts to hold them in.

The other gaped in dismay at the ragged stump of his right hand. The broadsword had cleaved through his wrist like butter, and the fingers of his severed hand still twitched as they clutched the stave.

Robyn and Littiljohn slid down the bank and confronted the knight. He stood at bay, the steel casque that covered his face swinging from side to side as he tried to keep all of his opponents in view.

"Stay back, Much," said Robyn as the big youth started forward, "or I will cut you down myself."

Robyn had dropped his bow and drew his sword. Littiljohn, who carried his massive stave strapped across his back, notched another arrow.

"Let him go," said Robyn. The moans of the injured outlaws were too painful to listen to, and he was suddenly tired of bloodshed.

His men looked at him in surprise, but obeyed and drew back. The Hospitaller remained where he was for a moment, wary of a ruse. When it became clear that they would not fight, he gave a contemptuous swirl of his cloak and stalked away through the woods.

Robyn rushed over to the boy who lay dying, his life-blood spilling from the fatal cut in his belly. Littiljohn and the others attended to his mutilated companion. With deft skill for such a big, clumsy-looking man, Littiljohn tore a strip of cloth from his mantle and wrapped it tight around the bleeding stump of the wrist.

"Gently, now," said Robyn, cradling the dying man's head in his arms, "peace, now, brave lad."

100

The boy's name was William Alton, he remembered, and he was from Newstead. He had tried to strike his blow in revenge for the destruction of his village, but picked the wrong enemy to fight.

Another name, Robyn thought bitterly, *to add to the roll-call of those who have died on my behalf. Another weight on my conscience.*

William tried to form words, but his mouth and throat were full of blood. The light slowly went out of his brown eyes as they held Robyn's gaze. His body went into spasm, and then with a final shudder his soul fled.

Robyn gently lowered him to the ground. For a moment he stared bleakly at the corpse, then brushed away his tears and stood up, filled with a strange resolution.

"We will come back, when all is done," he said, "and bury William in a Christian manner."

"Walter here is going to live – aren't you, boy?" said Littiljohn, patting the boy who had lost his hand. Walter's face was chalk-white, and he was clearly in exquisite pain, but he managed a nod.

"Much, take him back to camp," Robyn ordered in a stern voice. "We will speak of your folly another time."

The shame-faced youth obeyed, and helped Walter away.

Robyn and Littiljohn hurried back to the roadside. The sound of fighting had petered out, and they reached the verge in time to see the Hospitallers cantering away. The Italian crossbowmen jogged in their wake, still guarding the precious wagon and its crucifix. They left their dead and wounded strewn about the road.

"Finish off the wounded," said Robyn, and blasted the recheat on his horn while Littiljohn moved among the Italians, cutting throats with grim efficiency.

"That makes fourteen," he said when he was done, standing up and wiping his bloody dagger on his sleeve, "not a bad tally."

"It would have been more, if not for the Hospitallers," said Robyn. The wild charge of the warrior-monks had driven the outlaws back into the forest, giving the rest of de Sablé's men time to get away.

Summoned by the horn, Robyn's surviving men emerged from the forest. He did a quick head-count.

"Twenty-three," he said, slightly relieved, "it could be worse. Where is Thomas Alleyn?"

"Dead," answered Robert Cappe, a glover's son from Mansfield, "one of those damned crossbows got him."

Robyn bowed his head. Thomas had lost an eye trying to fight the dark knight, Gui de Gisburne, and had ever been a model of courage and loyalty.

Another for the list. How many more will die for me?

The treacherous thought crept into his mind. Robyn dismissed it. He could dwell on his guilt later.

"We will press on and shadow the Italians," he said, "keep to the forests, though, and only move within bow-shot when I give the signal."

He led his remaining men on, tracking the enemy through the woods like dogs on the scent of a stag. Robyn was aware that sending the wounded back to camp with escorts had weakened his strength, but the alternative was to abandon them. A more ruthless captain might have done so. The barons, no doubt, would laugh at his soft heart.

"Let them," he muttered, "I am The Hooded Man, not a soldier."

Soon the mighty donjon and soaring ramparts of Tickhill Castle appeared, rising over the trees to the north. Robyn's spirits sank when he saw the Plantagenet arms flying from the battlements. Once de Sablé got inside the walls, nothing short of an army could prise him out: a proper army, with miners and siege weapons, not a handful of outlaws and whatever garrison troops and peasant conscripts the barons had managed to hurriedly scrape together.

"We could pick off a few more of the buggers, before they reach the gates," said Littiljohn.

He and Robyn had climbed into the lower branches of a tree overlooking a slight dip in the road. From there they could watch the long, straggling column of soldiers marching quickly towards the castle. Robyn's ambush had given them a scare, at least, and he could see the men of the rearguard casting fearful glances over their shoulders at the forest.

"No," Robyn replied, shading his eyes, "that would mean quitting the shelter of the trees, and exposing our men to archers on the walls. I won't lose any more lives today."

"The priest has got away from us, then," Littiljohn growled, "again."

They watched in silence as the inquisitor, his mail shining in the late afternoon sun, spurred up to the barbican and demanded entry.

A slow smile spread over Robyn's face as the drawbridge remained shut. De Sablé could be seen engaging in a furious row with the men on the rampart above the gate. One of them was a tall, richly-dressed man whom Robyn assumed to be the constable. Their voices were too far away to hear, but the giste of the argument was clear.

"The constable refuses to let him in," Robyn said excitedly, "surely he cannot mean it? That is like refusing entry to the Pope!"

"Perhaps money has changed hands," suggested Littiljohn, "the barons may have bribed him to keep the Italians in the open."

That seemed the likeliest explanation, and for once Robyn had cause to thank God for the greed of noblemen. The constable of Tickhill clearly placed a greater value on earthly gain than the condition of his soul. No amount of threats or curses from de Sablé – the inquisitor could be seen gesticulating wildly, his smooth, childlike face enflamed with passion – could persuade him to open the gates.

Thwarted, de Sablé eventually left off haranguing the constable and returned to his men. For a time he conferred with the Hospitallers. Robyn watched anxiously, wishing he could overhear their discussion.

"Where in God's name are the barons?" he muttered, "inside the castle, perhaps? If they sallied out now, we could catch the Italians unawares."

De Sablé was nothing if not determined. Instead of turning back, his column moved off to the east, skirting Tickhill's high walls and following the highway north, towards Doncaster.

Doncaster was a large town, defended by ditches, earthen ramparts and a wooden palisade. "De Sablé could force entry to the town," said Robyn, "and then it would go the same way as Newstead."

"Fire and smoke," Littiljohn said grimly.

The outlaws followed, giving the castle a wide berth and working their way through the woods that flanked the highway to the east. They moved swiftly, careful to stay out of sight and hearing of the Italians.

Between the gaunt walls and towers of Tickhill Castle and the cruder defences of Doncaster there was a fair, open plain, divided by a river. Patches of woodland bordered the plain to north and west. The highway narrowed here, over some boggy ground south of the river, and crossed it via a wooden bridge, wide enough for two men abreast.

The barons had assembled their forces on some gently rising ground north of the river. Robyn's heart skipped at the sight of them. His eye made out the banners of Deyville and Ros, Everingham, Riparia, Fitzwalter and Percy flying among the slender lines drawn up beyond the bridge, among others he didn't recognise.

"I count one hundred and fifty or thereabouts," said Littiljohn as they crouched on the edge of a wood, "the Italians still outnumber them, but they have the advantage of ground, and the bridge."

Robyn knew he was no soldier, but tried to think like one as he studied the barons' dispositions. They had blocked the northern end of the bridge with a company of spearmen, some five or six lines deep. Peasant levies, mostly, armed with long spears and large wooden shields, their ranks stiffened by a few sergeants in kettle hats and brigandines.

Strung out either side of the spearmen were long, staggered lines of crossbowmen, protected by rows of sharpened stakes. Anyone attempting to approach the river and the bridge would have to brave a hail of darts.

"Deyville has chosen his position well," said Robyn, "the Italians would be fools to attack the crossing."

Drawn up behind the spearmen were a band of mounted

knights and sergeants. This made up the baronial reserve. Robin made out Deyville himself in the front rank, armed for war in helm, mail hauberk, shield, lance and sword. His comrades also bristled with weaponry.

Robyn expected the Italians to hesitate at the sight of such a formidable array, but reckoned without the power of faith.

De Sablé and his knights cantered onto the plain and took up position on a small hillock south of the bridge, well out of range of the crossbows. The mounted squires and sergeants slowly spread out into battle formation, directed by a stocky man-at-arms on a black mare.

"That's Fawkes de Lyons," said Littiljohn, "the King's captain of mercenaries. He came to Nottingham once, when I served in the garrison there. He has a good reputation. Competent, but not inclined to take risks."

"He won't like the look of this, then." Robyn looked at the defences again, and shook his head. "De Sablé must either withdraw or negotiate."

Last to come was the wagon. The team of horses pulling it were steered towards the middle of the Italian line. There they were unharnessed and led away.

What happened next was an extraordinary piece of theatre. The inquisitor rode up to the wagon, dismounted and struggled out of his helm and mail coat, revealing that he still wore his brown Franciscan habit underneath. He then climbed aboard the wagon, not without some loss of dignity, and stood in front of the giant crucifix.

De Sablé spread his arms wide, threw his head back and started intoning a Latin chant. His deep, sonorous voice carried across the plain and was taken up by his soldiers.

The effect was quite powerful, and made the hair on the back of Robyn's neck stand on end. In spite of all he had said and done, he had not quite shaken off a residual fear and awe of holy church, drilled into him from infancy.

If de Sablé hoped to intimidate the barons into surrender, he failed. Having taken up arms against the servants of the Holy See, they were not to be dissuaded by a few Latin verses.

The same could not be said for their followers. Robyn could

only watch in dismay as some of the peasants guarding the bridge broke ranks. Ignoring the shouts of the sergeants, they cast away their spears and shields and fled towards the woods.

De Sablé lowered his arms, and the singing abruptly stopped. A brazen peal of trumpets sliced through the air. His footmen swarmed towards the bridge, flanked by groups of crossbowmen, while the mounted sergeants and esquires charged towards the river on the baronial left flank, led by one of the Hospitallers.

The suddenness and ferocity of the Italian assault took the barons by surprise, as it had the outlaws in Sherwood. Deyville and a couple of other knights spurred forward, signalling at their crossbowmen to shoot.

"One volley," Littiljohn said nervously, "that's all they have time for."

The crossbowmen held their ground, knelt, and shot. Their darts wreaked havoc among the close-packed ranks of the charging Italians. Many horses and riders never reached the river, brought down in a chaos of flailing limbs and high-pitched animal screams.

Their comrades pressed on. The Hospitaller was struck in the shoulder, but he led a charmed life, and the dart failed to penetrate his mail. He urged his destrier into the river. She plunged up to her belly in the swirling waters, swiftly followed by the rest of the surviving horsemen.

"They cannot hold the bridge," Robyn exclaimed, punching the ground in frustration.

The spearmen north of the bridge, already weakened by desertions, could do nothing but crouch behind their thin wooden shields as the Italian crossbowmen took aim. Their darts punched through timber, cloth and flesh, felling almost the entire front rank. Brave men stepped forward to fill the gaps as the Italian sergeants, with a final war-shout, stormed across the bridge. Vicious hand-to-hand fighting broke out, both sides jabbing and thrusting at each other with their spears.

"Now's our time," said Littiljohn, rising, "we still have plenty of arrows. Let's knock over a few of the Italians on the bridge, and then close to take them in the rear."

Robyn was not so bullish. His senseless war-delight had long since faded, and he was determined to preserve the lives of his men instead of risking them in another brutal skirmish.

"Not yet," he said, knowing it sounded cowardly, "leave the barons to fight it out awhile."

Littiljohn frowned at him. "But they cannot hold. Look!"

He was right. De Sable's cavalry had splashed across the river and flowed up the opposing bank. Some of them had been unhorsed, their beasts rearing in terror as they tried to avoid the stakes, but there were still more than enough to drive back the crossbowmen. The Hospitaller was clearly visible, riding at will through the baronial ranks and doing terrible execution with his broadsword.

At the same time the defenders of the bridge were being forced back, buckling under sheer weight of numbers. The Italians seemed unstoppable, driven on by holy zeal, roaring their hymns as they stabbed men down and trampled them underfoot.

A rout threatened, and only prevented when the barons themselves charged into the fray. Deyville led one portion of his reserve against the Italian horse, while the Percies led the remainder in a desperate last-ditch charge to reverse the tide of battle at the bridge.

Still Robyn refused to intervene. As always, his men looked to him for leadership, but his nerve was fraying.

Someone had once told him that men were born with a finite store of courage. It steadily dwindled as they grew older and coped with successive crises. Being a young man, with a young man's high opinion of himself, he had scorned at the notion that he might one day turn craven.

It was true. His will and resolution had chosen this moment to desert him, now, when the fortunes of the day hung in the balance.

He looked at Littiljohn, and at the faces of his men, gathered around him. They were still eager to fight. One word from him, and they would gladly charge out of the forest and throw their lives away.

I did that, he thought, *I lit a flame inside them, but mine is snuffed out.*

He opened his mouth to order the retreat, but was rescued by Littiljohn. "My God!" the giant boomed, seeming to swell to a truly monstrous size in his rage, "do you lack the courage to finish what you started, then? I thought I had found a man at last, one I need feel no shame in serving!"

Littiljohn seized Robyn by the scruff of the neck and half-lifted him off his feet. "You will not fail us," he roared, his stinking breath gusting in Robyn's face, "do you hear me? I will snap your neck if you try!"

A second later, and the tip of Robyn's dagger pressed against Littiljohn's stomach.

"Release me," he said quietly.

Breathing hard, Littiljohn did so. They eyeballed each other, on the verge of blows for the second time in their short acquaintance. Robyn did not withdraw his dagger. In spite of his great size, Littiljohn could be murderously quick.

Mixed feelings of shame and fear drove Robyn to act. "We will attack," he declared, "aim your arrows at the Italians on the bridge. Forward!"

He stepped around Littiljohn and broke into a run, sheathing his dagger as he did so. His men uttered a shout and followed him onto the boggy ground just beyond the woods.

The Italian charge had been halted at the northern end of the bridge, where the barons dismounted and formed a wall of steel. They were heavily outnumbered, but mailed knights held the advantage over common spearmen in padded jackets. The Percies, uncle and nephew, held the centre of the line, laying about them with axe and mace. Still the Italians came on with appalling courage. Some were tipped into the river; others struck down and battered to death where they lay.

Robyn led his men to within bow-shot of the bridge. His fingers shook as he drew an arrow from the diminished sheaf at his belt.

"Damn," he cursed, fumbling the arrow as he notched it to the string. He bent to pick it up, notched again, raised his bow and loosed.

His men also bent their bows. The deadly iron-tipped shafts

sailed high into the air and dropped down onto the heads of the struggling mass of Italians on the bridge. They could not miss. Screams and gurgles mingled with the war-shouts and clatter of steel. More men dropped into the water, arrows sprouting from their necks and shoulders.

"Again!" Robyn cried. Another flight coursed through the air and claimed more lives. A horn blew at the northern end of the bridge, and the barons surged forward. The wavering Italians were shoved back. Panic rippled through their line, and a few of the men at the rear peeled away and fled.

De Sablé had held back a company of sergeants as a reserve. These men were now thrown into the fray. Fawkes de Lyons led half of them to shore up their comrades at the bridge, while the other half charged at the outlaws.

Robyn's fears dissolved as he plucked another arrow and took aim at one of the Italians, a stocky, bow-legged man with spear and shield.

The same calm he felt when hunting fell over him. His hand was rock-steady. He loosed, and the arrow hit his target exactly where he had intended, in the throat. The Italian dropped his spear and clawed helplessly at the several inches of wood and iron buried in his flesh. Robyn ignored him and switched to another target.

Littiljohn bounded past him, roaring like an enraged bear, wielding his massive stave. More outlaws followed, desperate to get to close quarters. Robyn remained calm. His second arrow took another Italian in the eye and pierced his brain. The man dropped instantly to the ground, stone-dead.

Now Robyn put down his bow, drew his sword and charged into the fray. The two sides met in the middle of the bog, sinking up to their ankles in wet mud. Ragged and helmeted figures hacked and stabbed at each other. The skies darkened and rain started to fall.

Robyn crossed blades with a better swordsman than himself. His opponent was taller and stronger as well, and drove him back with great sweeping blows of his sword. But this was a brawl, not a sparring-contest, and Robyn was full of tricks.

He deliberately dropped his guard. The Italian took the bait and unleashed a scything cut at Robyn's neck. Robyn dodged, spat in his face, kicked him in the balls and cut at him as he fell over. He missed. Cursing, Robyn kicked the Italian again as he tried to rise, trod on his spine and stabbed him in the back of the neck. Hot red blood sprayed up the blade and soaked Robyn's hands.

Someone slammed into his back and threw him down. Robyn twisted as he fell, yelling as he anticipated the cold kiss of steel in his flesh. Littiljohn loomed over him. For a moment Robyn thought the giant meant to kill him.

"Learn to guard your back," Littiljohn rasped, pointing his stave at the Italian who had been creeping up to knife Robyn from behind. He lay with his head smashed in like a rotten egg. The end of Littiljohn's stave dripped with his blood and brains.

"My thanks," said Robyn. Littiljohn stooped, grabbed his wrist and pulled him to his feet. More men came at them, shrieking for their blood. They fought back-to-back, guarding to right and left. Robyn fought on the defensive, clumsily parrying a host of spears and swords. Soon he was bleeding from any number of minor cuts and gashes. His companion's stave whirled in a lethal arc, cracking the skulls and limbs of any who came too close.

Robyn had no idea how the battle was faring. He fought for his life, sweat pouring in waves down his brow, mingling with the blood flowing freely from his wounds. His wrists ached. Every crash of steel against his sword numbed them further. The muscles in his chest, shoulders and arms were strained to their limit. His body was on fire with pain.

On fire…the inquisitor would burn no more innocents. Robyn would die before he allowed any more human candles to be lit in England. Summoning a last burst of energy, gritting his teeth against the pain and cramp, he beat down a spear and chopped at an exposed neck.

His sword carved deep into flesh and sinew and lodged there. A muscle tore in Robyn's shoulder as he tried to wrench it free. Blood spattered over his eyes, blinding him. The man he had killed fell backwards, ripping Robyn's sword out of his grip.

Robyn hurriedly wiped away the blood and drew his dagger.

He was almost too late to avoid the spear that stabbed at his breast, but managed to knock it aside. The Italian closed in, his blackish teeth and wild staring eyes just inches from Robyn's face. His strong hands seized Robyn's throat and started to choke him.

The Italian's eyes widened in shock, and their lustre faded. Robyn's dagger was buried deep in his gut. He fell away, screaming horribly. Robyn's hand was red to the wrist, but he managed to keep his grip on the hilt.

He had a brief respite to take stock. Rain was now falling in sheets and casting a grey curtain over the battlefield. He could see little save the silhouettes of men struggling in the murk, clawing and stabbing at each other. Bodies lay scattered about, their life slowly oozing into the wet mud. Those still standing were caked in blood and filth.

His throat was parched, adding to his long list of physical discomforts. Robyn bent double, gasping at the pain in his body and trying to work up some phlegm. The stench of death and terror and human excrement filled his nostrils.

"Are we winning?" he gasped, straining his eyes to see through the rain-mist.

Littiljohn paused in the act of beating the brains from a fallen opponent. "We're still alive," he said, "that counts for something."

Then they heard it: a fresh storm on the horizon, the thunder of hoofs and the screeching din of trumpets sounding the charge.

"Oh, Christ," moaned Robyn, "reinforcements. The inquisitor must have thrown in his reserves."

"But he has none," said Littiljohn, "save the Hospitallers, and there are too few of them to make such a racket."

Triumphant shouts rolled across the stricken field. Robyn and Littiljohn stared at each other in confusion. The knots of fighting men started to break up as one side cast down their weapons and fled.

Riders appeared through the mist, lances lowered as men ran like rabbits before them. Robyn strained to make out the arms on their surcoats.

A knight came thundering into view, bare-headed, his sword dripping with blood. Robyn thought he had grown immune to shocks, but one glance at the knight's face proved him wrong.

Eustace of Lowdham, High Sheriff of Yorkshire, had come to the rescue.

***

Most of the Italians died on the field, cut down in battle or the ensuing rout. Fawkes de Lyons and a good number of his mercenaries escaped to fight another day. The Hospitallers were slaughtered to a man, though not before taking a grim toll: four Yorkshire knights and fifteen sergeants lay dead around the scene of their last stand. Many more were injured.

Odo de Sablé refused to quit the field. Even as his little army collapsed around him, he remained standing before the great crucifix, calling down curses on the heads of his enemies.

When the battle was done, Deyville ordered some of his crossbowmen to drag the inquisitor from his perch and bring him before the barons and their allies. He regarded them all with lofty contempt, as though the fortunes of the day were reversed and they were in his power.

"Quite a coalition of the damned," he said, gazing without a trace of fear at the ring of weary, blood-spattered men standing around him, "kill me, heretics, and have done. I am ready."

Robyn stood apart from the barons, waiting expectantly for them to pronounce the death sentence. He had bound up his wounds, as best he could, but was still faint and had to lean on Littiljohn's brawny arm to remain upright.

To his astonishment, the barons hesitated. "There is no question of taking your life," muttered Deyville, their spokesman, "we merely sought to protect our interests."

Robyn lacked the strength to protest. He could guess what lay behind their reluctance to kill de Sablé. To fight against his soldiers was one thing, but to slay him, a priest and favoured servant of the Holy See, quite another. Their souls were already in jeopardy for this day's work.

De Sablé laughed in their faces. "Release me, and I shall

ensure that every one of you is laid under sentence of excommunication. Your souls shall be declared anathema, and cast into outer darkness."

At this moment Robyn realised that the barons truly were in his power. They looked cowed. None of them could meet the inquisitor's eye.

"Which one of you," he demanded, folding his arms, "is The Hooded Man? I take him to be some knight or baron, masquerading in the garb of an outlaw."

Robyn cleared his throat to speak, but Eustace of Lowdham got there first. "There he stands," said the Sheriff, pointing at Robyn, "and he is no gentleman at all, but Robert Hode of Linton and Loxley Farm, a Yorkshireman of humble birth."

All eyes turned to look at Robyn. His old lord, William de Percy, was absent having a wound attended to; otherwise the outlaw might have been identified already.

De Sablé made a choking noise, and his florid face turned ashen. "A peasant," he said, his eyes narrowing to slits, "an English peasant. This is the man who has humbled holy church."

"If you are humbled, priest," Robyn replied, "then you have none to blame save yourself. You might have made allies of these northern barons, and asked their help in capturing me. They are no friends of mine. Instead you forced them to take up arms to defend their rights."

De Sablé said nothing. His eyes were pin-pricks of purest hate. Robyn could almost feel the force of his hatred, and knew that this man would never cease hunting him until one or the other was dead.

"Now," said Robyn, deciding to twist the knife, "the servant of holy church has my permission to leave. You have been granted mercy, something you denied John Maker and all those other poor souls your men slaughtered for no good reason."

"Mercy," de Sablé spat the word out as though it had a foul taste, "I have no use for your mercy. It is an abomination. You are a foul perversion. The merest trace of fine feeling in you makes a mockery of God's creation."

For the first time in weeks, Robyn laughed. "That's right," he cried, clinging tighter to Littiljohn's arm, "I am a mockery. The trickster, they call me, and I laugh at men like you. You are a great fool, Odo de Sablé, and the Fool inspires mirth."

The inquisitor looked outraged, and the barons perplexed, which only made him laugh all the harder.

"If you won't put this poor fool to death," he said, "then do something worse, and humiliate him. Let him be stripped, tarred and feathered, and sent back to London strapped to a donkey. Let King Henry see that Odo de Sablé is but a man after all, and that the north of England cannot be ground under the heel of the Pope."

16.

The outlaws limped back to Sherwood, grieving over their losses, all the fight and spirit knocked out of them. Of the twenty-four who charged into battle, only fifteen returned.

Robyn had insisted on the dead being given a decent burial outside the grounds of a church near Doncaster. As a last favour, Deyville bribed the priest to perform the last rites over the bodies, even though they had died outside the law of God.

Eustace of Lowdham had arrived on the battlefield at a crucial moment with thirty mounted spearmen at his back, collected from the garrison at York. He might have arrested Robyn and his men, who were in condition to resist, but chose to set aside his duty.

"Here and now, Robyn Hode," he said, and Robyn detected the note of warning in his voice, "here and now. From sunrise tomorrow, we are enemies again. That should give you enough time to return to your forests."

Robyn had won a victory, of sorts, but it tasted sour in his mouth. Odo de Sablé was defeated, and the threat he posed to the safety of the north removed, but Robyn was still an outlaw, still destined to live like a hunted animal. He had merely staved off destruction, not avoided it.

His one consolation was the thought of seeing Matilda again. Thoughts of her dominated his mind on the trek back to Sherwood. He entertained wild thoughts of quitting the forest, and England, and taking her to some distant foreign land, where they could live in peaceful obscurity, unmolested by the law.

Such fond imaginings were shattered the moment they arrived back at the camp. A desolate silence greeted the outlaws as they filed back into the clearing around the Major Oak.

"Where in God's name is everyone?" said Robyn, looking around him. A throb of panic passed through him. There was something unnatural about the silence, and it felt as though they had entered a graveyard.

He snatched up his hunting horn and blew two quick blasts. The deep notes echoed and died away in the surrounding woods.

There was movement in the trees to Robyn's left. Two men emerged. One was Will, his face drawn and grey, the upper part of his left arm swathed in bandages. He leaned heavily on a stick as he walked. The other was Much.

"Still alive, then, Will," Littiljohn said cheerily, "I see they got that dart out of your shoulder."

Will stumbled, and would have fallen if Much hadn't stepped in and supported him. "The reeve of Applewick cut it out with a hot knife," he said in a wispy voice.

"The reeve?" said Robyn, "why didn't Matilda do it? She knows more about medicine and healing than anyone else."

Will was seen to make a great effort, as if steeling himself, and held a hand to his mouth before replying. "Robyn," he said at last, "it grieves me to tell you that Matilda is gone. She was taken by Adam of the Dale. He almost killed Tuck, and then took her away."

Robyn stood paralysed, robbed of speech. "Tuck lives," Will added, "though he drifts in and out. His head is broken, and there may be something damaged inside. The villagers of Applewick found him. Matilda was already gone by the time I returned."

"How do you know Adam took her?" demanded Littiljohn, "did anyone see him?"

Will slowly took a strip of parchment from his belt and handed it to Much. The boy lumbered over to Robyn and held it out to him.

Wordlessly, moving like a man in a dream, Robyn took the parchment and stared at the words hastily scrawled on it. Adam had carried a small supply of parchment, ink and quills, to scribble down melodies and lyrics as they occurred to him.

"It was nailed to the trunk of the Major Oak," said Will, "with his dagger."

Robyn was a slow reader, but the words gradually formed through the gauze of tears over his eyes.

If the Hooded Man wishes to see his lady again, he will come to the Watcher on the eve of the Feast of Saint Matthew. Alone, and unarmed.

The Watcher was an ancient lump of stone on a hill a few

miles beyond the eastern edge of Sherwood. There were all
kinds of stories about its original purpose. Some claimed it had
been a meeting-place for pagan druids, in the distant days before
the light of Christ reached England, others that it was a dormant
gateway to some hellish Otherworld. Whatever the truth, the
Watcher's glory had long passed. Time and weather had worn
the stone to a rugged stump, but it still radiated a kind of power,
and people preferred to give the hill a wide berth.

As dusk fell on Saint Matthew's feast day, a lone horseman
galloped towards the hill from the west. The surrounding
landscape was flat and largely devoid of cover, so anyone on
the summit could see the rider coming from miles off.

Robyn had brushed aside the protests of his men, and come
alone and unarmed, as Adam's message demanded. It was a
trap, any fool could see that, but he had no choice. He had gone
without sleep in the days since returning to Sherwood, and it
was a pale, hollow-eyed ghost that urged his courser up the
steep slope to the Watcher.

There were men waiting for him at the top. Two on horseback,
five more on foot. The footmen were soldiers, mailed and
helmed. They had crossbows, and levelled them at Robyn as he
wearily slid from his saddle.

"A man can stand against evil, sword in hand," he said, "only
to find a knife pushed into his back. I might have known that
treachery would do for me in the end."

He had recognised the horsemen instantly. One was Adam of
the Dale, though he had put off the patched and soiled clothes
of a wandering minstrel and swapped it for mail and surcoat. He
looked every inch the nobleman's son Robyn had suspected him
to be. His crisp fair hair and angelic features lent him the
appearance of some warrior-saint.

Adam's companion was much older. His battered, deeply-
lined face was familiar to Robyn, as were the quartered red and
white arms on his surcoat.

"I am sorry for this, Robyn," said Sir Fulk Fitzwarin, "it was
a mean trick, and not worthy of me, but there was no other way.
The king threatened to confiscate my lands and indict me for
treason unless I sent him your head."

Robyn had lent Fitzwarin four hundred pounds, so the knight could repay a loan he had taken out from the Abbot of Saint Mary's in York. Fitzwarin had needed the money in a hurry, to recompense the king for refusing to serve in the royal army in France.

"I thought it worth buying your friendship, Fitzwarin," said Robyn, "I was wrong. I was wrong about a great many things. So Adam of the Dale was a spy."

"I was," said the young man before Fitzwarin could answer, "and my true name is Fulk."

"My eldest son," Fitzwarin said, almost apologetically, "he insisted on playing the role of spy, even though I thought it dishonourable. It seems my sons have inherited my taste for adventure."

Robyn folded his arms and regarded them both with careless contempt. "Your honour," he said calmly, "is of slightly less value than the dogshit in Nottingham's streets. Where is my wife?"

"Safe and well," replied Fitzwarin, ignoring the insult, "she will not be harmed, I promise you that. But you will not see her again."

Fulk the younger signalled at one of the soldiers, who laid his crossbow down against the Watcher and drew his sword. Robyn glanced at the naked blade, gleaming dully in the fires of the setting sun, and knew his time had come.

"The trickster has been tricked," he remarked. "There is the making of a ballad in that."

"On your knees, Robyn Hode," said Fitzwarin, "for now you must die."

17.

Matilda woke up on a hard, narrow bed inside a tiny stone cell, and screamed. There was a searing pain in her skull. The scream only made the pain worse. She rolled off the bed and vomited on the floor.

Eventually the throbbing in her head relented a little. She paused, gasping for breath on her hands and knees, and tried to think. Dark clouds swirled in her brain, and piecing together a coherent pattern of thought virtually impossible.

The image of Adam of the Dale's face surfaced through the clouds. He had betrayed the outlaws, for God alone knew what reason. Killed or seriously injured Tuck, and taken her captive.

Matilda wiped her mouth and shakily got to her feet. She felt weak. Her dagger was gone. The door to the cell had a solid, cross-grained look about it, and was no doubt locked and barred from the outside. There was one narrow slit window which a child would have struggled to get through. Even so, a bar had been wedged in it.

Wrinkling her nose at the stench of vomit, Matilda leaned against the door and pounded weakly on it with her fist. "I am awake," she cried, as loudly as she could manage, "feed me, you bastards, whoever you are. I need food!"

She had some vague plan of overpowering her gaoler when he came in, even though she lacked the strength to overpower a puppy. The thought of being a prisoner enraged her. To be betrayed, and locked up inside four walls, was more than she could bear.

The door remained shut for a long time. Matilda was lying curled up in a stupor on the bed when at last she heard footsteps and the jangle of keys. A moment later the door swung open. Two monks stepped through, dressed in the black and white robes of Cistercians.

Matilda remembered Brother William, hung up like crow-bait on the tree overlooking Applewick.

"Is this revenge?" she asked, her mind still befuddled, "am I to pay for his fate?"

119

The monks had a gentle look about them, and didn't seem immediately inclined to harm her. "Peace, child," said one of them, "you have slept for two whole days and nights. Sir Fulk should not have hit you so hard."

"Sir Fulk?" The name meant little to her. She dimly recalled Fulk Fitzwarin, but he was an old man, and bore no resemblance to Adam of the Dale.

"Indeed. His father is here. He would meet you."

"Here? Where is here?"

"Rufford Abbey," replied the other monk, glancing with distaste at the mess she had made on the floor, "Sir Fulk the younger brought you here two days ago, slung over the back of a horse. He asked us to care for you, and to keep you safe until he returned with his father."

Matilda carefully swung her legs over the bed and sat up, clutching her head.

"Asked you, or paid you?" she said through gritted teeth. Matilda shared her husband's low opinion of churchmen and their motives.

Rufford Abbey. She strained to bring the place to mind. It was somewhere in Nottinghamshire, she knew that much. A spark of hope flared inside her. Sherwood Forest was not far away.

"My child, you should prepare yourself," said the first monk, who seemed of a kindlier disposition than his companion, "you have suffered a great loss."

"Come," said the other impatiently, "Fitzwarin is waiting, and I have no time to waste on comforting outlaws."

They shuffled out of the cell, beckoning at her to follow. Wondering at their meaning, but with a growing sense of dread in the pit of her belly, Matilda limped after them.

The cell opened onto a wide corridor, windowless and lit at irregular intervals by torches. Their footsteps echoed in the chilly semi-darkness. Matilda's head throbbed, until she had to bite her lip to avoid moaning with pain.

A flight of steps led up to a large, vaulted cellar filled with rows of wine barrels. The doorway of the cellar led to a long covered gallery. Matilda saw a garden to her left. A few monks in wide-brimmed hats worked in the late autumn sunshine, digging flowerbeds and removing weeds. None so much as glanced at her.

The Cistercians turned right and led her into a large hall, furnished with neat rows of polished tables and benches. A lectern stood at the southern end, for a monk to read out the lesson during meals.

Fulk Fitzwarin stood beside one of the tables. She remembered him clearly enough, and thought him a noble knight, one of the few to live up to his vows of chivalry.

There was a wicker basket lying on the table next to him. His rough-hewn face seemed to drain a little of colour when she entered. He placed one mailed hand on the lid.

"Matilda," he said, his voice echoing in the hall, "I am glad to see you alive. I feared my son had exceeded his orders."

Matilda leaned against the doorway. Her head swam. Nothing seemed to make any sense. "Your son?" she said, gasping at another stab of pain in her skull, "what do you mean? I have never met your son."

"That you have, though you didn't know him."

The hand resting on the lid curled into a fist. "I have to tell you that your husband is dead," he said, "slain last night, on my orders. I had no choice in the matter. The king had threatened to destroy me and my family."

Matilda might have taken this for a joke, but Fitzwarin's voice was harsh, and she could read the truth in his eyes. The pain in her head was as nothing compared to the invisible blade that now thrust into her heart and innards, over and again.

"I thought you should see him," he said while she fought for speech, "that much, at least, I owed you."

He flipped open the lid and thrust his hand inside. Matilda almost fainted as he seized a handful of hair and pulled out a severed head.

"This," he said sombrely, holding it up for her inspection, "is the King of England's price for my lands."

The head had reddish-brown hair, a curling beard, and her husband's long, slightly gaunt features. It bore more than a passing resemblance to the man she had loved.

It was not, however, the head of Robyn Hode.

END NOTE

Robin Hood is one of the most famous and enduring of medieval legends, but this work is based on history: a man named Robert Hode or Hood, nicknamed 'Hobbehod', really did fall foul of the law in Yorkshire in 1225. At the same time another outlaw, a notorious criminal named Robert of Wetherby, was at large in the same county. I have made these basic facts the building blocks of my tale.

Please do get in touch if you have enjoyed *Robin Hood (II): The Wrath of God.* It is always pleasant to receive feedback from readers. The next episode, *Robin Hood (II): The Hooded Man* is in the pipeline, and for those interested in the real history behind the tale I would recommend Robin Hood by J.C. Holt and The Outlaws of Medieval Legend by Maurice Keen.

Follow David at his website:
davidpillingauthor.weebly.com

Or contact him direct at:
Davidpilling56@hotmail.com